ONE YEAR AT YUMA

EN

—

ONE YEAR AT YUMA

When John Benedict hit Roger Mondell for maligning his sister, he was in deep trouble. Roger struck his head on the mantelshelf and lay there dead. Labelled as a murderer, Benedict fled to the Caribbean.

However a few months later he was back in Texas and heading west. But Mondell's cousin Louis made a vow to find and kill him. Benedict soon found himself locked up in a hell-hole called Yuma Prison—a sitting target for Louis Mondell.

ONE YEAR AT YUMA

by

Amy Sadler

Dales Large Print Books
Long Preston, North Yorkshire,
England.

British Library Cataloguing in Publication Data.

Sadler, Amy
  One year at Yuma.

  A catalogue record for this book is
  available from the British Library

  ISBN 1-85389-620-9 pbk

First published in Great Britain by Robert Hale Ltd., 1994

Published in Large Print February, 1996 by arrangement
with Robert Hale Ltd.

Dales Large Print is an imprint of
Library Magna Books Ltd.
Printed and bound in Great Britain by
T.J. Press (Padstow) Ltd., Cornwall, PL28 8RW.

ONE

As the man in the plain black suit walked up the main street of Benson leading a brown horse with a white blaze down its nose, his gaze took in the signs denoting what the small town had to offer. It seemed much the same as those he had already passed through since he had stepped back on to his homeland soil about six weeks ago. There was a sheriff's office and jailhouse; a few small shops; a couple of saloons and eating places, one showing the speciality of the day at fifty cents. He noted a general store to his left with a ramp running along one side of it through an alleyway to a back street. Diagonally across from the store was a building with a sign which had slipped at one end that said, Mercantile Bank.

Heat bounced up at Jonas Buckland from the hard rutted street. It was close

7

to noon so he decided he would see if there was a room at the two storeyed building with hotel painted on it, which had a balcony extended across it above. He was weary from travelling and although the vast arid terrain had held him frequently awestruck, he had also experienced depths of depression and loneliness.

As he turned to lead the horse to a hitching-rack, his thoughts were on a large glass of beer. A sudden commotion up the street caused him to pause and his eyes took in the three men who came rushing out from the bank. There was a pistol shot inside the bank. Two of the men rushed to their horses tethered some yards further up on the right. The third man somewhat behind was firing at another in the bank doorway. A shot from a rifle way up the street made him swerve. A rider who had just been about to tie up his horse had seen quickly what was taking place. His second shot hit the man in the leg and he stumbled only a few feet away from Buckland who stood rooted. A small linen bag flew out of the man's hand and skidded to land at Buckland's feet. It was probably a natural reflex that caused him to stoop and pick it up.

At the time of the first shot Deputy Sheriff Hatcher was sitting in the office reading, rather laboriously, the latest news sheet. He raised his head. It was not usual for anyone to be firing off at this time of day. Certainly not in recent months. He got up and reached for his gunbelt and quickly fastened it on. Sheriff Riggs was out visiting a rancher and would doubtless be staying to partake of a good meal. Another shot made him move himself quickly to the street. He looked up to where the sounds were coming from and saw the man down and two others trying to scramble onto their mounts. He saw the man standing with something in his hand, saw him suddenly take off for the alley. 'Jesus, it's a bank raid!' he exclaimed in amazement, as he could now see two of the clerks on the boardwalk outside the bank, one of them firing a pistol.

Pulling his Colt, Hatcher got off a shot at the man who had dived for the alleyway, then another at the limping man who was trying to get himself off the street. Buckland, on realizing he was in great danger of being shot, yanked the reins and ran for the alleyway by the store. A bullet from the rifle shooter almost grazed his face as it went past and plunked into the side of the store.

Hatcher on seeing the clerks had taken care of the stranded man who now lay in front of the store bleeding to death, took off in a hurry running down the street to a cross section and legged it fast through to the back street, turned right and headed to cut off the man with the horse.

Buckland was almost through when he saw the man with a star on his vest, gun in hand coming at him. He turned to back up.

'Hold it right there. Don't you make no sudden moves you scum, or I'll blast you.' Hatcher yelled.

Taken by surprise, Buckland was struck dumb for some moments as Hatcher came cautiously towards him. It came to him then that this lawman believed he was one of the robbers. He had his hand across the saddle with the bank bag in it.

'What you got there?' Hatcher came forward.

The horse jumped and backed up and was forced up against the ramp, disliking Hatcher's aggressive manner. Buckland tried to quieten the horse, and just then the bag slipped from his hand falling close to the back hoofs, then as Hatcher reached for the horse's cheek strap with his left hand, it scuffed the bag under the ramp, snorting and rolling its eyes.

'Listen, I'm not with those men,' Buckland said angrily to Hatcher.

'Shut your mouth and put your hands on your head. Where's your piece?'

'I haven't got a gun. It's the truth what I'm telling you.'

'The bag, where is it? You had one of them bank bags in your hand, I seen it!' Hatcher yelled.

Buckland put his hands up. 'I dropped it. It's here somewhere,' he said, becoming really worried.

Hatcher dragged a pair of manacles from

his back pocket. 'Stand still, you damned thief.'

Buckland moved. Hatcher hit him over the head with the gun butt and Buckland sagged against the horse.

Out in the street the two bandits still alive were being brought in by the rifleman, Dick Hinckley, who worked at the livery, and Sheriff Riggs who had cut off the fleeing men as he was coming up the trail. One had a leg wound, the other was in bad shape having been creased across his left side. They were helped into a cell at the rear of the sheriff's office.

When he came round some time later, Buckland found himself in an iron barred cell, with a gash across his temple and blood down the side of his neck. Why was he in here? He saw the other two men, one stretched out on a bunk and moaning, the other holding a bloody leg as he sat on a chair.

A man with a star on his vest whom he saw was not the one who had hit him, was telling someone to go and fetch the doctor.

Buckland called to him. 'Hey, I'm not with these two. Why am I in here?'

Sheriff Riggs, a thick set man with greying hair, a bushy moustache, a weather burnt complexion and a pronounced limp, turned and asked crossly, 'What the hell you talking about?'

'I was just getting out of the line of fire when I went into the alleyway. I had just come into town.' Buckland explained agitatedly.

'Oh sure! I guess it was some other fella my deputy and Al Jessup saw picking up that bank bag your compadre threw to you.'

Buckland spluttered. 'I never saw these men before. I told you, I had nothing to do with the hold up.'

'Well I know who they are. They're the Bedford boys. They've been robbing banks for quite some time. All over the place from Colorado to Mexico and now they'll do plenty of time at the Yuma Prison. That'll quieten 'em down some,' Riggs said crossly.

The deputy returned then with the

doctor who on examining the man laid on the bunk said, 'I'll have to have this one removed to my surgery to get the shell out of him. I reckon he's got a fifty-fifty chance.' He bound up the other's leg which had a flesh wound. Then he looked at Buckland's head and dabbed it with Iodine.

Lem Bedford, the eldest of the three brothers, was carried across to the doctor's office, while Art sat looking miserable on the bunk.

'Why don't you tell the sheriff I had nothing to do with the robbery? That we have never met before.' Buckland pleaded with Bedford.

Art Bedford was still thinking about the foul up. Thinking about his younger brother who'd been killed. Why should he help this bastard who had tried to make off with the bank bag after Bill had dropped it?

'Shut up! You got yourself into this trying to make off with the dough. Sneaky bastard!' Bedford growled.

Buckland went silent. He was in a

bad fix and was completely innocent. What if the sheriff should learn who he really was?

Sheriff Riggs went to pick a bottle of whiskey out of his bottom drawer after the doc had got two men to carry Lem Bedford over to his office. He took a long swig. His leg, that had been broken when his horse had fallen on it while out in a posse, was bad today and giving him hell.

Julian Bevis, the bank manager, came striding in, a bandage on his wrist which he had twisted while trying to get at his revolver in his drawer. He looked pale and worried.

'Sit down, Julian, have a snort,' Riggs invited him. 'You got a count on what was taken?' He looked hard at the harassed-looking man.

'They took three bags. If it hadn't been for Dick Hinckley, they'd probably have got away. Two of them anyway. Billy did well too. It was lucky you were on your way back. The bank will be giving out a reward. I'm not sure how much the Bedfords' are worth. I've

15

done a tally. Fortunately the ranchers and some mining companies had drawn out their payrolls. They'll be relieved. I make it fifteen thousand dollars, quite a considerable loss, of course, had they got away.'

Riggs got up and reached for the two bags from his desk drawer. 'I haven't touched it at all. I was waiting for you to come and check it. There's only two bags though.'

Bevis looked startled. 'I'm sure they took three!' he said and emptied the bags out on to the desk. After he had counted it he looked rather pale. 'We're over half short,' he said and began to sweat.

Riggs looked embarrassed. 'Jed said the man he caught in the alleyway had been holding something in his hand and Jessup said he saw him bend down and pick something up when the one who was killed dropped what looked like a bank bag when he stumbled.'

'Then where is it?' Bevis looked aghast. 'Where is Hatcher? Get him to go and make

16

a thorough search,' he almost screamed at Riggs.

Hatcher came running from the street when Riggs shouted at him. 'There's eight and a half thousand short. That geezer must have planted that bag someplace afore you got to him.'

'I been looking. I can't see it anywhere. He must have shoved it somewhere in that alley. I'll go through his things too. Maybe I should go in there and beat it outta him.' Hatcher shouted at them. It looked bad for him. Bevis, he knew, had little regard for him.

Riggs said. 'I'll go through his things that's on the horse. You search that alleyway again. Get help if you can.'

Bevis went off to the bank with the two bags which had been recovered, and Riggs went through Buckland's carpet bag. There was clean underwear, two spare shirts, shaving tackle. Soap and towel. A Colt .38 and spare ammo. A bedroll with spare pants rolled inside with a ground sheet. In one of the saddlebags were some dried fruit hard biscuits. A pair of lace-up shoes of good quality. He checked the saddle and blanket beneath. Nothing had been stashed in there. It was a complete mystery. As Hatcher had said, he must have slipped the bag somewhere. But where? He went back inside and through to the cell. 'You!' he spoke to Buckland who was sitting on a bunk in abject misery. How could he have got himself into such a predicament? What would happen to him if they would not believe he was not a robber? He got up, looking astonished, as Riggs asked him, 'What did you do with that bank bag? Where did you stash it?'

'I did nothing with it. I don't know why I picked it up. It was just a reflex. I was going to take it to the bank. Then bullets were flying all over so I ran into the alleyway. You can see I don't have it. Your deputy must have picked it up when I dropped it. He wouldn't let me explain. Then he hit me.' Buckland told Riggs.

'You must've slipped it somewhere. You had time I reckon before Hatcher got round to the back street.'

'I tell you I did not put it anywhere. I

let it fall when my horse was playing up when the deputy came raging in at me. You should ask that man there. He knows I've never seen him before today. I was on my way to get a room at the hotel when it all happened. I'm not used to this kind of thing.'

Riggs looked frustrated and turned to Art Bedford. 'Was he in on it? Is he part of your gang?'

Bedford snarled. 'Go to hell!' You can't do no more agin me.'

Riggs turned back to Buckland. 'What's your name?'

'Jonas Buckland. I have papers on me to prove it. You must believe me. I had nothing to do with the raid.'

Bedford gave a guffaw. 'He sure enough picked up the money bag, sheriff'

'Shut up you piece of garbage. You and your brothers been robbing banks and stage lines for years. There's a thousand apiece on your heads. Dead or alive!' Riggs spluttered at him angrily. He was frustrated over the missing bank bag and wondering about Hatcher. He stalked out

19

just as Hatcher came back.

'No sign of it. I done searched that alleyway from end to end. I looked underneath the ramp. Under a water barrel and the spouting. Went up the steps to Jessup's loft. Nothing, nada! I reckon Bevis has made a mistake.' He looked somewhat expectantly at Riggs. 'You want I go work them two in there over? I'll find out if they was working together, and where that damned easterner stashed it.'

Riggs gave him a look of scorn. 'We won't be doing no beating up, not while I'm sheriff. He do talk like an easterner. Maybe he is telling the truth.'

'I did hear once that the Bedford boys used some one to work out the raids for them. Someone smart. It could be this fella is the one. They chuck the loot to him, then when a posse catches up with 'em, they got nothing on 'em.'

'Buckland told me you caught him in the alleyway not in the back street.' Riggs looked hard at Hatcher. 'I don't know why you need have hit him if you had him cold there and so near the office.'

'He's a lying skunk! I got him at the end and there was some Mexicans going down the street. He could've tossed it to them.' Hatcher lied. He was in a bad spot. If Riggs thought he'd taken the bag, then Bevis and others might soon start thinking that way.

'Well, if they did get it we'll never find it. You could search them adobes till kingdom come and find nothing. They could keep it for months, spending a bit at a time or whoever got it will be long gone over the border in no time. That's if they got it. I'm going to see doc and see if the other one is still alive. You hold the fort and don't go harassing them two back there. Let them stew a while.'

Doc Hughes looked up as Riggs came into his back office. 'How is he?' he asked looking at the man stretched out on an old sofa.

'Oh, I think he'll make it. I got the bullet out. He's in pain, but if he stays quiet...'

'He'll get at least ten years,' Riggs reckoned.

21

'He won't last long if he gets sent to Yuma Prison.'

Riggs nodded. 'Well, it's out of my hands now. Judge Hamish is tough and he'll be here in about two weeks. Bedford can be brought back to the cell when he can be moved, Frank.'

'I'll keep him a while. He's not likely to try anything. I've given him laudanum. It'll be touch and go a day or two, then he should mend,' Hughes said.

Buckland lay on the bunk. The deputy had brought food for him and Art Bedford. He was now seriously worried. The deputy had taunted him, and the other disagreeable character who lay opposite him moaning about his leg had a nasty odour about him. Hatcher had laughed in a gleeful manner when he had asked him about his horse.

'I'll take real good care of him. You won't be needing him no more. Not for a long time. Judge Hamish will see to that.'

'You know perfectly well I'm no robber. I think you know where that bank bag is,' he'd flung at him.

22

'You stick to your story, Buckland. Nobody ain't going to believe you. That fancy eastern accent won't carry no weight with Hamish. He don't much care for dudes like you.'

Of all the things to happen, Buckland thought. It was six months now since he had fled to Jamaica, six difficult lonely months. If he hadn't punched Roger Mondell he wouldn't have hit his head on the mantel shelf in the ale house. Murderer they had called him. Roger's drunken pals. His uncle Henry Mondell would, he was quite sure, have sent him to jail for life on a trumped up charge. There was no love lost between the Benedicts and the Mondells. Even his father could have done little to get him off. A charge of manslaughter would have got him twelve years with Judge Mondell on the bench. He'd had no choice but to run. Any decent fellow would have done what he had done, if he had heard his sister's name being maligned as Roger was mouthing off in his drunken fashion. It had been lucky one of his father's ships had been in port and the Captain had got him away safely to Jamaica. He would not see his sisters, nor his parents perhaps for years now. He could not have risked going to jail. It would have finished him. Now here he was in almost the same predicament, in danger of going to a hell hole of a prison in Arizona, alongside all kinds of renegades, murderers and, worst of all, no one would know where he was.

So far, no one had gone through his pockets. He had a money belt with a thousand dollars in it and the papers he had bought in Jamaica. Legitimate papers bought from an English sea captain who had buried a man at sea, of almost his own age. It had cost him all the money his mother had scraped up that night before he had gone aboard the ship. His father had been away at the time and he hadn't seen him. He had managed though to get money to him by another of his ships' captains. He had also had a letter from him telling him who to contact as a go-between when he got back on American soil.

After coming ashore at Matarosa on a

coastal vessel from Cuba, he had made his way by stage-coach to El Paso. There he had run into some difficulty with two disreputable characters and been goaded into a brawl, and had been on the receiving end of heavy punishment in a saloon until a youngish rancher had drawn his six-shooter and settled the fighting in a matter of minutes. He had then spent a week at the ranch of one Cliff Rawlins, and bought the horse from him and a Colt .38, after Rawlins had given him some concentrated instruction in how to use it. He had owned his own horse since a youngster and knew well enough how to ride. The western saddle had been awkward at first, but now he was used to it. He had never before been west of the Carolinas, and at twenty-six had been ready to settle down and marry.

According to Captain James, his father's trusted friend, everyone in Baltimore believed he had fled to England, which was in his favour. America was a big country and he was prepared to start a new life with his new name, till the day things settled down and his father might visit him and decide what to do.

Hatcher came in and interrupted his thoughts. 'You two can go out back if you want before I lock up,' he said. 'Don't try running. I'll drop you if you do.'

When they came back in Bedford asked Hatcher if he had any liquor. 'I ain't going to sleep with this damned leg hurting so bad.'

'You got a nerve! The bank manager hurt his wrist. How do you think he feels? And your brother? Might croak before the night is done.' Hatcher cackled.

Bedford swore at Hatcher in a cold hard voice and told him what he would do to him when he got out.

'You'll get ten years, Bedford, only most don't last more than two or so in that hell hole. Cemetery is full of men like you.'

After they were locked up again, Buckland said to Bedford, 'It's best not to say anything to him. It only makes him worse.'

'He's a mean bastard. If we had tried to run out there he would have shot us both. You can be sure of that. I reckon he was hoping we would. I robbed a few banks but I ain't never killed nobody, only in self defence. I'd kill him if I only had the chance. He's worse than we are, and him a lawman.' Bedford snarled.

Buckland lay on his back, his head aching from worry and the gash Hatcher had given him. He felt like bawling. If only his father were here to get him out of this mess he was in. Bedford was right, this deputy was worse than he was, hiding behind a lawman's badge. Getting away with his foul deeds. He was quite convinced he had hidden the money some place and, more than likely, would disappear one day with it.

TWO

Sheriff Riggs was doing justice to a large portion of apple pie at Ed's Eats when Hatcher came striding in.

'You better come, Ben, the circuit judge

has jest arrived,' he said grinning fatuously.

Riggs looked up. 'Well, take him to the hotel, he'll want to freshen up. Tell him I'll be there as soon as I can. Hamish won't be doing much today but sleep, I reckon.'

Hatcher looked agitated. 'It ain't Judge Hamish, it's a young fella. Name of Wallace and he's come from Phoenix.'

'Don't get yourself all in a dither. Just do as I say. He'll be needing a rest if he's come all that way. See he gets a good room.'

Riggs finished his pie and coffee. Hamish was getting too old, he thought. Be an improvement if this one ain't so cantankerous. He got up and dropped some coins on the counter and went over to his office. At least this Wallace fella was early. Now he could be rid of his three prisoners. He moved the dirty mugs off his desk. Why in hell don't Jed ever clean this place up, he thought, irritably. Wish I could be rid of him, he treats the prisoners like they was dirt, especially Buckland. Riggs had had doubts about his deputy since the bank raid. Buckland could be telling the truth. The Bedfords weren't saying if Buckland had or hadn't been in it with them. Jessop had witnessed Buckland's dash for the alleyway, and seen him pick something up. Buckland wasn't in the same class as the Bedfords, he seemed to be like one of the upper class moneyed lot. There was something of a mystery about him though. Doc had talked with him and spent more than usual time on looking at his wounds when he came to see Lem Bedford.

Buckland had insisted on being taken to the bath house every day, but Hatcher had cut that to twice a week. Prisoners were entitled to some privileges. It was better to have someone like Buckland who kept himself clean and had his shirts and underwear washed. Even the Bedfords, after seeing the advantage of getting out for half an hour or so, had copied him.

Hatcher had kept a very close watch on them, but Lem Bedford was in no shape to do much. Art had a leg wound. It would go hard on those two in the Yuma Prison, Riggs thought. How would

Buckland cope? Well they shouldn't have gone on the outlaw trail. Most of these renegades ended up stopping a bullet or going to jail in the end.

As Hatcher came in Riggs got up from his chair. 'He satisfied with his room?' he queried.

'Didn't say nothing. He seems more of an educated type. Got a good suit on and one of them real nice leather cases for his papers, I guess.'

Riggs gave a brief smile and went off to the hotel. He went up the bare wooden staircase and knocked on the door at the far end of the corridor. A voice said 'Enter'.

Wallace was putting on a fresh white shirt over his vest. The room smelled of toilet water. Riggs coughed. 'I'm Sheriff Riggs. I hope you got every thing you need. Will you be wanting to see the prisoners today?' he asked, taking in the fresh faced man who was probably in his late twenties.

Wallace smiled. 'May look in today sometime later, Sheriff. Right now I'd really enjoy a beer, would you care to join me?'

Riggs nodded. 'Surely!' he said affably.

Wallace, still a bachelor and thirty-two years of age, and something of a ladies' man, was fair haired, handsome, with a small moustache, and about six feet tall. He had finished law school at Harvard and then moved west with his parents and two sisters and a younger brother to settle in Phoenix. He knew the Territorial Governor well and had taken on this job of circuit judge when Judge Hamish had suddenly had a stroke only two weeks ago. The experience he thought would be invaluable, and he looked forward to the travelling, to get to know the territory.

Riggs took him to the best saloon where he ordered two large glasses of beer and they went over to a corner table. Wallace drained down the glass and put up a hand and called for two more. By the time they'd sunk two pints apiece, sweat was coming out of Wallace. He was feeling the heat and he turned to Riggs to say. 'I'd like the hearing to be set for tomorrow at nine thirty. If you can have six impartial men ready for the jury, we can get the matter settled. I'll go and rest now and look in later to see the prisoners.' He excused himself and Riggs took off for his office, his thoughts in motion about who he would pick for the jury.

When Doc Hughes popped into the jailhouse after he had seen Hatcher go off to the rooming-house where he boarded, he greeted Riggs in a rather subdued tone. 'I suppose those three will be gone in a day or two. I hear the judge is a new young fellow.'

'Yep! Seems a decent sort. A proper educated lawyer from the east. Can't say how he'll be!' Riggs looked speculatively at his old friend.

'Perhaps he won't be so hard as Hamish,' Doc said gravely. He was most unhappy about Buckland. He believed him to be innocent. After Lem Bedford had been put into the cell with Art, Buckland had been placed in another cell. He had had a chance to talk with him while treating the gash on his head. 'Listen, Ben. Buckland says I can have his horse to look after if he should get sent to prison. It does look bad for him. Jessup and others too are sure he was in on it. Buckland doesn't want Hatcher to get the horse. I'd be glad to take care of it.'

'You know well enough, Frank, prisoners lose most of what they have. The warden will take their money and clothes. Watches, anything like that. Or the guards, for bribes to get 'em smokes.'

'Put me on the jury, Ben,' Hughes said, looking pleased at the idea.

Riggs sat thinking a while then he looked at doc. 'All right! Only don't make it look like you're too eager. I gotta have Jessup as a witness, and Hatcher, unfortunately.'

'I wouldn't trust Hatcher out of sight,' Doc said coldly. 'The way he treats the Mex folks is a disgrace. You ought to get rid of him.'

Riggs coloured. Doc was his friend but he did not like being told how to run his business. There were witnesses who had seen Buckland pick something up and which was believed to be the bank bag.

'I reckon Judge Wallace will get it sorted out. It won't be the first time some upper class fella got hisself into trouble. If I let Buckland go the folks will be on my back. There's the election soon and I figure on taking another term or two yet.'

Hughes sighed. 'I doubt we'll ever know where that money went. What really happened in that alley. Only Hatcher knows that!' Doc got in a last shot.

Hughes went through to see the prisoners. At least he would be paid for his time. It would make up for those bills that never got paid. He never pushed those who were poorly off.

Buckland had not slept well since being incarcerated. Tomorrow he would know his fate. Doc Hughes had been good to him and heard his side of things. But there was nothing he could do. Doc came in with a cheery smile on his face. He sat down and pretended to look at the gash which had healed up. Two weeks they had been locked in the jail and Buckland felt stiff and sore all over. He pushed his hand down inside the lining of his jacket and pulled out a small roll of paper money. 'Doc, take this just in case they don't believe me tomorrow. There is a thousand dollars. I've kept a little just in case. I want you to have my horse if the sheriff will let you have it. I don't see why he shouldn't. Say it's for payment for treating me. I had the money, it is nothing to do with the bank raid. I do not need to rob banks. If you can get me some paper I will write a letter which I want you to post for me. If they do send me to prison,' he said miserably.

Doc hesitated, then he slipped the money into his black bag which Hatcher always insisted in going through if he was in the office, in case doc might slip in a pistol. Riggs never bothered.

Doc got up to leave. 'Good luck tomorrow,' he patted Buckland on the shoulder. 'I'll take care of this and the horse. I'll bring the paper in later,' he said and left in a hurry.

Riggs had ordered a specially good meal for the three men. In Yuma they'd get nothing but pig slop. Buckland would come in for some bad treatment not being one of the usual types, most being murderers, rapists and bandits. He felt truly sorry, even just a little for the Bedfords who were silent now the judge was here. They knew they'd most likely get ten years at hard labour for their crimes of robbery.

Hatcher was also glad he'd be rid of his charges soon. Buckland's eyes were always on him, accusing, cold. He hated the easterner. Even though he had told Riggs he had come from England via Jamaica, he still believed he was guilty. They would knock the shit out of him at Yuma. There was something of a mystery about that geezer and no doubt about it. He went through to collect the plates. Lem Bedford spoke in a hoarse and quietly menacing voice. 'I reckon it's you as ought to be going to that prison. You ain't nothing but scum! You better remember us. We'll be out one day, and then we'll be coming for you. We like to pay our debts.'

'You'll get ten years. If you ever survive

that hell hole, you'll not be fit even to walk out.' Hatcher threw back at them and walked off.

Buckland stood at the bars, his knuckles white. He said nothing. He just stared after Hatcher.

'I'll slit that bastard's throat, so help me!' Art Bedford snarled.

'Best to say nothing now,' Buckland said. 'He'll be on the witness stand. The judge will be watching us. Anyway, Hatcher will get his one day, I'm sure.'

Lem Bedford nodded. 'I reckon he will,' he said.

By 9.15 a.m. the room used for council meetings and dances and such was crowded. Six men were seated at one side, amongst them was Hughes. Behind a table sat Judge Wallace with a law book and a pitcher of water and glass, and his gavel. He shuffled some papers and cleared his throat and asked the sheriff to send in the prisoners.

Hatcher hustled the three men in, Lem Bedford looking pallid and needing help to the bench where they sat down, their wrists manacled. Hatcher stood behind them and was wearing two Colts and carrying a rifle. There were two more men outside similarly armed, just in case.

To Buckland this was the final insult. He had never felt so humiliated or degraded. Then it would probably have been the same in a Baltimore court if he had stayed to face charges of murder or manslaughter. But at least his family would have been there to get him the best possible lawyer. Here he had none. He stared straight ahead wondering if God was punishing him, though he was not of a religious nature.

It did not take long to deal with the two Bedfords. They had been caught after robbing the bank. They did not deny it and pleaded guilty. They did not however plead guilty to attempted murder, and denied it vigorously. Wallace took note that they had never been involved in murder, as far as was known.

As there was no lawyer to act for Buckland, and after checking with Riggs, Wallace considered his case more carefully.

He let him speak without interruption to tell his side of the event. Yesterday while at supper he had had a visit from Doctor Hughes who had given him the facts, as near as he could, though he had not been a witness during the raid. He had told him exactly what Buckland had told him and that he believed he was innocent. The fact that the missing money had not been found, Wallace thought, was something of a mystery. He was inclined to think the deputy knew more than he was telling. The fact that Buckland had been knocked out for some time was the key to how and when the money did disappear, and would obviously never be known. It might well be that Buckland had made a pact with the deputy. But he would hardly be likely to set himself up for a prison sentence. None of the witnesses would swear under oath that it was a bank bag they saw Buckland reach down and pick up. He needed more time to consider this particular case. He rapped the gavel down hard. He looked at his watch. It was 11.30 a.m. 'We'll adjourn for an early luncheon,' he told an

39

amazed sea of faces. 'I need more time to assess the case of Mister Buckland, and to decide on the sentences.'

The courtroom was abuzz with conjecture, annoyance and debate about the new young judge. 'He's got to go look at one of his law books, I'm thinking,' Jessup reckoned. 'Hamish would've had 'em on the train this afternoon,' he added somewhat scathingly.

The prisoners were hustled back to jail by Hatcher and Dick Hinckley who was assisting him; Hatcher in a foul mood because the judge had cut him short once or twice when he'd offered his opinion too readily.

The saloons did brisk business. Ed's was overflowing as was the cantina. Doc Hughes went home for his meal feeling more hopeful. His wife gave him an amused look. 'I don't know why you have got so involved, Frank,' she said dishing out a plateful of ham hock and vegetables.

'I don't like to see injustice done. Buckland might have something to hide but he's no bandit, of that I'm sure. A sensitive young man such as he. Well it'll kill him in Yuma. Break his spirit. He won't ever be the same, if he survives it. Those other two knew the score. Knew how it might end one day.' Hughes spoke emotionally.

At two o'clock the courtroom was packed full again. Wallace took his seat after having had some words with the jury in a back room.

The judge's clerk a local council member called the court to order. 'Will the two Bedfords stand up please.'

Lem leaning on Art, a lot of pain in his side waited for the verdict.

'What is your verdict?' Wallace asked of an elderly greying man who led the six.

Jack Stanton, with a piece of paper in his hand, read out what they had agreed upon. 'Lem and Arthur Bedford be both guilty of robbing the Mercantile Bank of fifteen thousand dollars. A sum of eight and a half thousand not yet recovered. Since it was their dead brother Bill who fired at the bank clerks, we can't rightly accuse them of attempted murder. They let off some shots, but we can't rightly say they fired at anyone in particular.' Stanton sat down again.

Buckland stood up next, grim faced and shaking inside. He badly wanted to go to the toilet.

Stanton got up again. 'We believe Jonas Buckland to be guilty of taking up the bank bag as is missing. In view of the lack of evidence as to what happened when he went into the alleyway, we can only reckon he was guilty of trying to abscond with the bag. On listening to his story, we can't rightly say he ain't one of the Bedford gang, nor that he is. I guess he saw a chance and took it.'

Wallace nodded, he was pleased with the way the jury had responded to his guidance during the recess. He had bought whiskies all round, not the most ethical thing to do. In Baltimore it would probably have got him disbarred, but out here he believed these people needed a little pushing towards less biased views.

'All prisoners rise,' the clerk announced. The room went deadly silent.

Wallace spoke with quiet authority.

'Lem and Arthur Bedford, you are hereby sentenced to four years at hard labour and will be henceforth transported to the Yuma Prison.'

There was a concerted intake of breath, some 'oohs' and 'aahs'. Hatcher looked absolutely stupefied.

Wallace called for quiet. 'Jonas Buckland, you are hereby sentenced to one year at hard labour, also to be transported to the Yuma Territorial Prison. The court will now rise.' He got up and left the room.

Buckland sat down hard. There was a brief show of relief on his face as he mopped the sweat off his brow with a rather soiled handkerchief.

When Hatcher heard the sentence he shouted 'No!' and took his hat off, throwing it onto the floor in a rage. 'That judge has been got to. They should've got ten years!'

Riggs came over to him. 'Jed, shut up before Wallace hears you and cites you for contempt of court, and gives you a heavy fine.'

'Buckland should've got same as the

43

Bedfords. It's because he's an easterner like Wallace.'

'Get the prisoners back to their cells and be quick about it,' Riggs said angrily.

Prodding them unmercifully, Hatcher, with Dick Hinckley assisting, got the prisoners back to their cells. Then pulled a bottle out of a desk drawer, mouthing off obscenities against Wallace and the jury.

Doc Hughes felt a great relief at the sentences. One year was not so bad, but at Yuma even a year would be pure hell. Some men he knew, got into things out of desperation when they couldn't find work. He had talked a little with Lem Bedford who had had to take care of his brothers when both their parents had died of influenza. Breaking rocks in the Arizona heat was something he shuddered at. He went after Riggs to have a word with him. 'How long before they go?'

'Oh, a day or so. I gotta make arrangements and get the paperwork ready.' Riggs answered him briefly.

'You'll not send Hatcher, I hope?' Doc

looked worriedly at the sheriff.

Riggs gave doc a shrewd look. 'No, I reckon not. I guess Brewer could use a buck or two,' he replied.

THREE

It was three days before the Bedfords and Buckland were escorted to the station in a wagon, closely guarded by Hatcher and the two sworn-in deputies, Sam Brewer and Nolan who worked at the mortuary but had often been called for posse duty. Hatcher gave a last spiteful prod at the three prisoners as they were led up a ramp into a stock car then the door was shut. A short time later the train got up steam and departed. Buckland sat with his back to the solid end and gazed through the rails as the countryside moved past them. The Bedfords sat a few yards away and the two deputized men further up the car, their rifles close to hand. The sliding door was padlocked on the inside and Brewer had the key. He saw no difficulty in getting the three men to Yuma. He had done several years as a sheriff and was now retired and living off a few acres of land with his wife. His two children were grown and had left home when they'd married. The easterner, he thought, looked ready to bawl. He didn't know how lucky he was that Judge Hamish hadn't been able to continue his work. Hamish was a mean old hypocrite in his book. He had once found him carousing, in a drunken state, with three Mexican girls; one of them he had sent to jail for a month some time later, for stealing a few apples from the store.

Buckland had his bedroll and carpet bag with him and he was seated on some straw which smelled highly of cattle dung. He was glad to be out of the jail. It had seemed he had been there for ever. This brief smell of fresh air was a welcome break. He knew though from what he had heard there was much worse to come.

Doc Hughes had given him a tin of salve and he'd hidden his few dollars at the bottom. It was a risk but the only place he could think of to hide it where they might not search.

'They'll not let you keep much,' Riggs had told them. 'Your soap, towel, but not the razor or a knife.'

He managed to write a letter to his father's associate in Los Angeles whom he had arranged as a go-between for correspondence, and doc had promised to send it off for him.

'If I don't come when I get released, keep the horse and the money,' he had told the good doctor.

As the train trundled along, Buckland thought about Hatcher. How long would it be before he would be tempted to spend some of the money? A considerably nice piece of money. Most likely he would resign in a few months and take off somewhere. He despised him. The Bedfords were better than he. They had probably resorted to bank robbery out of desperation. Jobs were scarce, especially out here in the west, and particularly if you were illiterate. Feeling sorry for the Bedfords eased his own self pity somewhat. Why he should feel sorry for them, he wasn't sure. They had been of no help to him. He fished in the paper bag that doc had thrust at him as they were brought out of the cell, and which Hatcher had searched thoroughly, growling his displeasure. There were six hard boiled eggs, some bread and cheese and a few apples. He picked out an apple, then he looked across to Art Bedford. 'Would you like an apple?'

Bedford hesitated. 'Sure, it'll be the last I reckon for some time.'

Buckland tossed it over to him. Lem was already sleeping so they did not disturb him.

The motion of the train soon put all of them to sleep, except Nolan who kept himself alert by humming softly and smoking. The train stopped at Tucson and Brewer got out to refill their two spare canteens. 'Why didn't you fetch us a nice big beer?' Art Bedford asked grinning.

'Maybe at Casa Grande. You got two bits?'

'Sure, I still got a buck or two, my own

not the damned bank's. I reckon Riggs was a decent type, he let us keep what we had. Hatcher would've took it if he'd been sheriff. One day I'll be calling on that piece of scum,' Art said bitterly.

Buckland had been watching the terrain. The huge saguras, cholla and other cacti completely fascinated him. Brewer gave him the names of many of the variety he could see as they moved along in the heat of the day. When they got to Casa Grande Nolan went to fetch food and some bottles of beer. The train was fairly slow. It was dark when they finally got to Yuma.

The door was opened by Brewer and a wooden plank slammed against the car. The three went down it, tension making them awkward and apprehensive. A sheriff and two deputies were there to greet them and soon they were incarcerated once again in a cell. Brewer and Nolan handed over the paperwork and told them goodbye, wished them luck, and departed for the hotel. Sheriff Baker gave them some coffee and a mutton sandwich apiece. 'They'll be picking you up in the morning,' he

49

said briefly and left them in charge of a deputy.

They were up early and given a decent breakfast. All three were silent. There was nothing to say.

At eight o'clock a wagon rolled up with an iron cage on it, and they were led out and handed up into it. The gate was locked and the two guards who were heavily armed clicked up the horses and drove right down the main street. A few pedestrians gave them hard uncaring glances. The prison loomed before them up on a hill. The wagon was let in through a heavy door of the stockade and went across a hard packed square that threw up heat during the day.

During the next hour they had had their clothes taken from them and replaced with the grey prison clothing, and fitted with leg irons that had about a yard of chain between each iron. Then they were taken to a cell which was dug into the side of a rocky bank where four three tiered bunks were back inside and in darkness when the iron barred hessian covered gate was slammed shut and padlocked.

Buckland sat down on the lower bunk of the first tier. The two Bedfords took a lower and middle one opposite, only about a yard between them.

'We're like moles in here!' Art Bedford wailed.

'They don't treat animals like this,' his brother said hoarsely.

Buckland was too shattered to speak. They had let him keep the tin of salve, his spare underwear and towel, and soap. His good shoes and boots were gone and replaced with a pair of old sandals. The guards had been rough and coarse. They had taken little notice of Lem Bedford's condition. It was cold in the cell. The bunks had straw pallets only and one miserable blanket which was threadbare and smelled. The whole place stank. A year of this, he would be finished. And what of the other two? Four years. It would drive them mad. No wonder so many died, as Hatcher had mentioned.

It must have been hours before anyone came near. Then it was to bring them out into the square where they waited in the scorching heat till a heavy set man came. Around forty or so, Buckland guessed, with thinning hair a square jaw, and pale blue eyes. He introduced himself as Warden Pike, and gave them a lecture on what they could or couldn't do. Tomorrow they would join the work gang breaking rocks. He gave Buckland a raking stare before he walked off. A guard let them have some water and told them they would eat when the work team came back at the end of the day.

The sun had gone down when the work team were brought back. They were allowed to wash at a trough then were the first to eat, the meal consisting of large chunks of bread, a bowl of what was described as stew and a mug of thin coffee.

Buckland, the Bedfords and others who were too sick to work, or did chores around the prison, then got what was left.

'First chance I get when I'm feeling better,' Lem Bedford told his brother, 'I'm out of here, even if I get shot trying it'll be better than four years in this pest hole. This food...hell, a hound dog wouldn't even look at!'

When they got back to the so-called cell, they found four more men inside. Three were Mexicans and had taken the front bunks where Buckland and the Bedfords had been. There was an altercation till one of the Mexicans spoke up in good American. 'We should not fight amongst ourselves, the guards will come and they will beat you hard with those sticks they carry. They might throw a snake or a scorpion inside. You must watch out for these,' he said evenly.

Buckland spoke up. 'I'm sorry, we didn't know if there were others in here. You are right, we ought to stick together. I'm Jonas Buckland,' he said and put out a hand to the man who stood a foot away.

'Felipé Fernandez, only everyone calls me Hawk,' the Mexican said and struck a match on a wall.

The Bedfords moved to the next tier where a man who had said little, growled and said. 'I'm sure glad I got some better company at last. You got any tobacco?' Sol Clemens asked.

'The guard took what I had,' Art told him.

At Fernandez' suggestion, Buckland took the middle bunk leaving the bottom one free. 'Things crawl in. It is better to be away from the ground, though the ceiling is also to be looked at. We have a guard who is not so bad, his name is Collins. He brings matches and does not hit us when the others are not around.'

The night was long and cold. They were up at sunrise eating more bread and drinking the brown liquid that passed for coffee. Then they were lined up in the square and sectioned off for the wagons. Buckland stuck with Hawk who he had talked with a little last evening. He was glad to have someone articulate to talk with. This Mexican seemed to be in the same predicament as himself. He had been caught stealing a chicken. He had come across the border to escape being shot by the Federales. He had been hungry. The homesteader had handed him over to a sheriff who hated Mexicans. For stealing a chicken the judge, equally bigoted, had given him two years.

He had done only seven months. In the daylight, Buckland could see how thin he was, the eyes sunken. The guards delighted in prodding the Mexicans with the yard long round sticks they carried, as well as their rifles or side arms.

They were loaded into the iron barred wagons and taken more than a mile to a small canyon which was wired up at both ends. Once they were inside a gate was padlocked. Guards stood around with rifles. One or two rode up on the rims with rifles slung across their backs. There was a hut at the outside of the gate where the guards could brew coffee and take turns to rest in the heat of the day. The men were allowed one hour at noon time and given more bread and water, sometimes fruit, depending on how the guards felt.

Lem Bedford collapsed during the first hour. A guard kicked at him and Art went for him. Jake Collins was standing close to them at the time and gave Art a quick rap over the head. 'Stay out of it, or you will be put in the hole in solitary,' he whispered.

'Lem was shot, he ain't fit enough. It'll kill him and open up his wound,' he told Collins.

Two more guards came over and Collins suggested that Lem could sit and hammer at the rocks that were already loose. They were then put into wagons and taken to the railroad where they were hauled off to where they were needed for laying tracks upon.

Buckland was with Hawk breaking up the larger rocks with a sledge hammer. In no time he had blisters and a headache. He used his handkerchief after tearing it in half to bind round his hands. He was not sure how he lasted the day out and by the time he got back to his pallet flopped on to it in despair. Later he sat up and put some of the salve on to the blisters. He could have hugged Doc Hughes. He called up to Hawk. 'If one has money, do they let you spend it on things?' he whispered as Hawk looked down to him.

'Collins will get things for you, if you have money, but be careful. You must hide it.'

'Where? I have some money,' Buckland whispered.

'Give it to me. I have a place up here I dug out in the wall, but I have nothing now to hide.'

Buckland hesitated. Then he passed up the tin of salve. 'Here, it's in the bottom. Please use the salve if you want some,' he offered. He also handed up the soap.

'Sunday is the best day to talk to Collins. They let us stay out in the yard. You can wash your underclothes and get a haircut if you can pay. Most cut their own with knives they have hidden. There is one man to stay clear of. He is known as Bull. That is his given name. Even the guards are afraid of Bull. Never let him catch you behind any of the larger rocks in the rock pit. It is surprising what he can get away with. You should warn your two friends not to become friendly with him, especially the younger one.

Buckland felt himself blanch. What Fernandez was suggesting, he had not thought of before. Never in his life had he felt so demeaned, so utterly miserable. Thank God for Hawk. He at least gave him a little comfort with his friendliness.

The next morning there was something of a commotion by the next cell. Collins was speaking loudly to one of the prisoners. 'Give me a help with the stiff.'

Fernandez whispered to Buckland, 'Muerto!' Buckland knew French. He gasped. 'Someone died!'

Hawk nodded. 'It is not unusual. It is Cannon, he has been here a long time, he is old. I am happy for him. He is better off dead.' He spat into the ground.

The long nights in the stinking cell were the worst for Buckland. He was getting used to the hard work breaking rocks, and at least was not so stiff and sore. Being allowed out in the yard was a real treat so he could wash his underwear. There was no hot water, but he managed to get it clean. Most prisoners who had been in for a long time had no change of clothes. Once a month the prison suits were washed but they never got back the same set. Sometimes the trousers were too short. The worst thing was the sores round the legs, and the terrible food. How could they expect men to work on such rubbish? Buckland wondered. Hawk had told him the warden probably took half the money he was allowed for the rations.

Collins came over where he and Hawk were seated, their backs against a water barrel. 'You, Buckland! You got any money stashed?'

'Why do you ask? You know they took everything off me when I arrived,' he answered angrily.

'I can get you smokes. Maybe some fruit. If you managed to hide some of your dough. I can do it now while Drago and his chums are in town.'

Hawk nudged Buckland. 'Do it. Collins is OK.'

Buckland gave Collins two dollars after he had slipped back to the cell and fetched it. Collins fetched him a bag of tobacco and some papers and a small melon. He also had bought some cheap tequila and let Hawk and Jonas have a little. It burned their stomachs and they coughed. They sat in the sun after rolling the smokes and felt a little better.

The next day while in the rock pit, Jonas went over to ask Lem Bedford how he was, as he thought he looked on the verge of collapse.

'It's the heat. I can't stand it. My wound ain't so good.'

'You, what you want here?' Drago's voice made Buckland jump.

'I was concerned about Lem. He isn't fit to be in this rock pit. He should see a doctor.'

Drago hit Buckland across his back with the heavy stick. 'It ain't none of your concern. Get back to work afore I lay you out.'

Buckland swore at Drago. 'You're worse than these prisoners. You should be breaking rocks. You...'

The stick came down hard right across Buckland's shoulders and he let out a yell. He could hardly straighten himself up. He was sure a rib was broken.

Bull had been watching from a spot just above. He came down shouting obscenities at Drago. 'You scum bag. You leave the dude alone or I'll break your back.'

Drago went for his side-arm. 'Get back, Bull, or I'll put one in you.'

Collins had come up then and spoke quietly to Buckland. 'Go now, get on with your work and stay out of sight some place.'

Buckland lurched away, as Collins stepped in front of Bull. 'Go on back, Bull. You don't want to get yourself shot,' he said evenly.

Bull did as he was told. He had only intervened because he had seen Buckland and the breed smoking yesterday, seen Collins sitting with them. The new fella must have money. He would ask him for

61

tobacco for saving him from going to the hell pit, which was in a tunnel with only a small hole giving air at the top. One day in there was terrifying. He'd spent a week in there when he first came to Yuma. The next time four guards had tried to put him in there for fighting, he had almost killed one of them and injured two so seriously, one had resigned his job, and the other had been in hospital, which was only a shack, for a week. Now the guards mostly left him alone.

The next morning Lem Bedford was left out from the work party. He helped out in the cookhouse with easy chores, and managed to snitch a few things which he took to the cell and shared around. He and Art had more respect for Buckland from then on. They even spoke to the Mexicans in more friendly vein.

Bull approached Buckland while they were eating their evening slop. 'I see you got tobacco. I reckon you owe me for today,' he said smiling as if they were now the best of buddies.

'I had a little. I shared it with my

cell mates.' Buckland told him rather off-handedly.

'When Bull does a favour, he expects one back,' the big broad-shouldered, heavy-bicepped man's eyes went cold, as he glared at Buckland.

'All right, Bull. Tomorrow I will give you two cigarettes. I do not have the tobacco on me now. I am grateful you put Drago in his place,' Buckland gave Bull a dismissive look and got up from the bench he sat on at a rough topped table under a tin roofed awning, and walked off, or rather shuffled in the fashion he had adopted since wearing the leg irons. He felt anything but calm inside. He was quite terrified that Bull would come tearing into him and throw him down, or break his arm or a leg.

Buckland was something of a hero in his cell. He had somehow managed to face Bull down. On the other hand they were afraid Bull would await his chance and do something to Buckland. Lem Bedford was quite concerned. 'You just watch out for Bull and Drago. And Drago has pals. He

63

snitches to Pike, so the cook told me.'

'Don't worry, Lem. Let me see that wound. I'll put some salve on it. You stay in that kitchen as long as you can.' Buckland advised Bedford.

Art Bedford sat watching as Buckland put the salve on his brother's wound. 'Christ! I never thought I'd be chumming up with a gent like you,' he said almost in tears.

'Don't put too much faith in our friendship, Art. You could have helped me in Benson, but you chose not to.'

Lem spoke up. 'Honest to God! We thought you was helping yourself to our dough, what we got from the bank. What Bill...if he hadn't let go of it...'

'Yes, if! It's a little word but it covers a lot. If only you hadn't chose to rob the bank the day I rode into Benson. None of us would be here in this stinking lousy place.' Buckland snarled and went to lie on his bunk. How in hell was he going to last a year out in such appalling conditions?

When Sunday came, Collins asked

Buckland and Hawk if they would like some company. Mexicans girls he told them. 'Two bucks apiece. Take 'em to the cell.'

Hawk looked with disdain at Collins. 'No thanks! I don't want to get myself full of disease. It's bad enough trying to survive as it is!'

Art Bedford looked interested. 'I ain't had a woman in weeks. But I ain't got two bucks,' he muttered.

Hawk laughed. 'When you've been in here a month or two, mi amigo, you will not remember what it was like, I can assure you.'

'Jeez, what about after four years!'

'You won't have nothing left by then, pal,' said Collins.

Buckland gave a sigh. It had been months for him too. But he had little inclination in that direction. After a day in that rock pit, he was so tired, sore and burnt, women were the least of his worries. There must be a way to escape and run for the border. 'Has anyone ever got out of here?' he looked at Collins.

'One or two, they found their bodies in the desert. Picked clean by the buzzards. Some try to run, if they get chance, just so the guards will shoot them and get it over with.'

'What about bribing the warden?'

'He'd take dinero, that's sure. But it'd have to be quite a lot. He has his job to consider. To promise him dough wouldn't work. He would want it in his hands.'

'It's almost impossible to get to see him,' Hawk put in, sounding bitter.

'You gotta start a riot,' Art Bedford opined. He had been listening carefully. 'I know a fella who got out of a prison by setting it on fire. Everything they could lay their hands on.'

'Wouldn't work here. Not in those rat holes. The guards would pick you off in seconds,' Collins said. Forgetting momentarily he was a guard. He had once been an inmate and because of his good record and hadn't long to go, Pike had let him become a guard when two had quit and another been killed.

Collins got up as he saw Drago letting some girls out through the stockade gate. 'Don't do nothing stupid you lot,' he called to them and walked away.

FOUR

Hatcher was fit to be tied after the prisoners were gone. He watched the inhabitants of Benson like a hawk to see if anyone was spending more than was usual, especially the Mexicans and the good doctor. He was particularly chagrined that Hughes had been allowed to take care of Buckland's horse.

Hatcher was not the only one wondering about the missing bank bag. A certain Louis Mondell was also considerably intrigued. He had read about the bank robbery in a Tucson newssheet. He had stopped off there after he had first gone to Brownsville and Matarosa to make enquiries about one John Benedict who had been seen boarding a vessel at Havana which was bound for the gulf coast. The picture in the paper of the three miscreants at first had not been of much importance to him until he had noticed the likeness of the man called Buckland, to John Benedict. No wonder the Benedicts had not denied rumours that their son had fled to England. It all made sense now. John had gone to Jamaica where the Benedicts had a sugar plantation; most likely on one of their ships. Then gone to Havana and on to Matarosa and come back on to American soil again. More than likely with a set of papers and a new name.

Fate was giving him a hand. Had he not seen the paper he would be on his way to Los Angeles instead of heading back to Benson. The thought that his brother's killer was now in some prison, or perhaps breaking rocks in heat such as he had encountered in the past week, gave him a great deal of satisfaction. The drooping moustache had fooled him, but on closer scrutiny, he felt sure this Buckland was none other than Benedict. He must make certain though. One year and he would be free again. That's if he lasts, he thought, maliciously. The type of men he would be incarcerated with would be the lowest of the low.

When he got off the train at Benson, he was immediately spotted by Hatcher who kept a close eye on strangers who stopped off in his domain. He at once tagged Mondell to be an easterner. When Mondell actually stopped to ask him if there was a hotel, he even offered to carry the black leather bag and escorted Mondell right to the small reception desk.

Mondell, however, was not unaware of the deputy's ingratiating attention and thanked him coolly for his help and took the key for his room and went on up the stairs. He was hot and tired and keyed up. He needed to rest before he set about making a few enquiries.

At the time the robbery was taking place in Benson, young Sandy Bullen, only five years of age, was searching for his pup and had just located it at the rear of Jessup's store. He had it in his arms and was about to retrace his steps to his home some 200 yards away when the first shot rang out. The pup leapt out of his arms and skiddled in under the store which was about two feet off the ground to let air flow under it. Sandy dropped down and scrambled under after it calling for it to come out. The mongrel pup was cowering and whimpering away under the ramp by the alleyway. Sandy crawled on his belly in the dust and got to it and grabbed its back legs hauling it to him. He could hear more shots being fired. It wasn't usual of late to hear gun fire at this time of day, he thought. He could also hear voices shouting in anger, and one he recognized to be Hatcher's. He seemed to be trying to make someone give himself up.

Half scared and excited at the same time, Sandy wished he could get out to see what was going on. He pushed himself further forward towards the ramp and could see a horse's hoofs scuffing up the dust and men's boots. The horse seemed frightened as it pranced, then suddenly something came skidding under the ramp almost in front of Sandy. It had gone very quiet in the alley and the gun fire had also stopped. The pup yelped as Sandy squeezed it against him as he reached for the beige coloured bag. He got himself turned around and headed back and came out at the far rear corner of the store. He got up, placing the bag between the pup and his chest and ran on home as fast as he could.

The Bullen house was a three bedroomed clapper board structure with a small bit of garden in front and a barn and sheds at the rear. Sandy ran up to the room he shared with his older brother, who with his sister was at school, and dropped the pup and bag on to his bed, and got his wind back. Then he opened the bag and looked inside. What he saw took his breath away. It looked like money and lots of it. Where had it come from? Who had dropped it? He could not read the writing on the side of the bag which said Mercantile Bank. He sat thinking for a while, then he remembered what his late paternal grandpa had once said when he had found a silver dollar in the street. 'Finders is keepers,' that's what he said. Sandy grinned. Now I got a secret from Jim. He don't tell me his secrets. I'll hide it. I can buy everybody nice presents at Christmas, give 'em a real surprise. I'll buy myself one of them catapults like Danny MaGraw has. He took a ten dollar note from one of the wads and shoved it in his pocket. He could say he found it, if anybody asked where he got the money from to buy the catapult.

Quickly he ran downstairs and out to the barn. He thought of Jim's old hiding place for his secret collection. He didn't use it any more now, so he got on to the straw bales and using them as a ladder, he shoved the bag in under the roof by a strut. Grinning he got down again. 'You and me's got a secret,' he told the pup as it sat wagging its tail.

At the back of the barn Jack Bullen was coming out of his quiet contemplation. He was wont to stop off for a half hour's rest before his wife called him in for dinner.

She was over to the Ransomes doing a spot of cleaning for them. Lucky folks who could afford such a luxury, he thought. Bullen had spent all morning ploughing his piece of land where he grew melons and beans and such. The rear of the barn was the coolest place in the midday heat, where he had a bottle or two of beer stashed in a bucket of water, and for which he had something of a penchant, and which reduced his income considerably.

When Bullen heard the scuffling over to the far corner, he lifted his head in something of a daze and was not entirely sure what he thought he saw. Getting up slowly he walked across to his son as he came scrambling down. 'What you been stashing up there, boy?' he said rather sternly.

'It's my secret, Pa! Jim has secrets, so don't you tell him,' Sandy said earnestly.

'I won't tell Jim. Now you show me what you just put up there.'

Sandy looked sullen. Then he saw his father was serious and reluctantly climbed back and brought down the bag.

Bullen saw the writing on the bag and gasped. He opened it up and dropped the contents on to the floor. Kneeling down, he let out his breath with a rush. 'Where the hell you get this, boy?' he spluttered.

'I found it, Pa! It's money, real money isn't it?'

'You know damned well it is! Not that you ever seen a whole heap. By God, I never seen so much at one time, neither! Where did you find it?'

Upset because his secret had been discovered Sandy began to whimper.

'Don't cry, boy. I ain't going to whup yer. Just tell me where you found it and when.'

'Can't I keep it, Pa? I would like to have my own real secret from Jim.'

'Sandy, I'm waiting. You tell me now and be quick, afore your ma gets back.'

'I was under Jessup's store getting Chip. I heard some shooting and a lot of noise in the alley way. I stayed under 'cos I didn't want to get shot.'

'Go on, boy!' Bullen said intrigued.

'There was a hoss and it kicked

something under where I was so I brung it home when it was quiet again. You remember what grandpa once said? Finders is keepers. So I reckon I found it, so I can keep it, can't I?'

Bullen stood a moment then he put his head back and laughed till tears ran down his face. 'Listen, Sandy. I gotta do some thinking about this. And I gotta find out what's been going on. You put that bag back up there, and you say nothing to anyone, you hear me? It'll be our secret. Yours and mine. Now you spit on your hand and promise. We'll shake on it, and you don't ever tell anybody, you understand what I'm saying?'

Sandy saw the seriousness in his father's face. He was impressed. To have a real big secret with his pa was the greatest thing as ever happened to him. 'No, Pa! I'll never tell anybody, honest!'

They spat on their hands then shook them in a firm grip. Then they could hear Constance Bullen calling them to come get their dinner. She was full of the bank raid. Bullen gave his son a sly look and shook his head. 'I'll go see Jessup later,' he said and got on with his dinner.

Later that evening Bullen put the bank bag in the bottom of the grain bin, well covered. He had given the whole thing a lot of thought, and what Sandy had said about finders is keepers, he had dwelt on for some time. The banks had a whole heap of money, they would not miss it. He had counted it out and sat a long time thinking. He could buy a nice piece of land back in Iowa where his wife's folks lived. It was almost ten years since he had deserted the army. No one would be looking for him now. No one would recognize him, he felt sure. He could get out of this arid heat ridden country. Constance would be pleased. The kids would have a better chance. If he sold up what he had, it would pay the fares and some left over. He had saved a couple of hundred. Nobody would be surprised if they left town. In a month or two after he got his last crop up. The story about the fella stashing the money someplace seemed odd. Maybe Hatcher knew where the money had dropped. He hadn't said so though. What if he had seen Sandy grab it? The best was to wait and see and listen to the gossip. He could always hand it in later, if Hatcher seemed suspicious, say he never knew Sandy had hid it. He had worked his ass off for the army and got a pittance for it; the country owed him. Running about after lousy stinking Indians and they'd been fed food worse than pig swill. Yes, he would keep the money, he decided.

FIVE

Marcus Kingsley looked at the envelope that had been placed on his desk and had strictly private written across it. It had been franked in Arizona which puzzled him. When he opened it he found three pages inside covered in small writing. It began: Dear sir—and the signature was by someone called Frank Hughes. He read the letter through quickly. So, John Benedict was in Yuma. Of all the messes he could have got himself into. This was as bad as could be. John was his godson, he must do something to help him. After reading the letter through again, he pulled paper towards him and wrote rapidly. John senior would be devastated. Of all the rotten luck, to get young John away then to be put in jail for something he didn't do. After he had copied out the letter from Hughes and written another of his own, he placed them into an envelope and put a seal on it. Then he put it into another strong envelope and addressed it to Captain Hector James at his Baltimore residence. The retired sea captain would then take it to his associate John Benedict. Perhaps he would think of something that could be done.

Kingsley wrote two more letters, one to Frank Hughes and one to the prison warden at Yuma, to see if he might make a visit to see his nephew, Jonas Buckland. It would carry more weight, he thought, if he said John was his nephew. He then went personally to see the letters were to be despatched as soon as possible. It would be hard on young John in a place like Yuma. He had heard the rumours of how bad it was.

When John Benedict senior received the letter about his son, he was devastated. His first thought was that he should go to Arizona. After reading the letter once more he decided it too great a risk. It was certain Mondell would send someone after him, or follow him himself. The reason he used James for correspondence about John was that he thought his mail might be tampered with. Louis Mondell would be up to such treachery. Thinking quickly, he sent a note round to the lodgings of a certain Paul Devane, a private detective he had used once or twice and whom he trusted for his discretion.

Two days later Paul Devane joined Benedict on board one of his ships that was unloading at the docks. They talked for more than an hour after which Devane accepted the assignment. It sounded to be the sort he relished and was better than collecting evidence on a certain husband's nefarious activities.

After giving the aggrieved wife the evidence he had collected, he made his preparations. He packed his nankeen pants, wool shirts and leather jacket. His Colt .45 and the latest Winchester rifle, and a thin bladed knife he had been given by a Mexican renegade when he was down in Sonora searching for the misguided son of a wealthy politician.

He arrived in Yuma a week later having taken precautions against being followed. He got himself a room at the hotel which was located at the corner of a street. The town was hardly a place to endear one to it. There was the prison on the hill; a fort, which had but a few blue coats keeping an eye on some Indians on a reservation up the river. The journey had been tiring, dusty and hot. It was early October, the sky blue and not a cloud in sight. After rinsing off the grime he went to find an eating house and managed to dispose of tortillas and frijoles, and some melon. He then bought a bottle of whiskey and went back to his room. When the bottle was half empty he tossed off his outer clothing and lay on the bed under a quilt. He put his revolver, his knife and money belt under the pillow and went to sleep. After twelve hours of uninterrupted sleep, he got up and washed himself over and put on the western clothes. After a late breakfast of bacon, eggs and hot cakes, and lots of coffee, he went to the livery stable to hire a horse.

Devane lay on the crest of a small jagged ridge as a few clouds appeared on the southern skyline. He was using his powerful field glasses which he had focused on the rock pit where some hundred or so prisoners were breaking rocks. The heat was still fierce at three in the afternoon. God alone knew how those men kept themselves upright day after day hammering or picking out those rocks. Devane had seen a similar scene in Mexico, and had narrowly escaped being captured and condemned to a life of such labour, or until he had dropped dead. 'Sure and be God, if ever I should be in such a fix,

I'd do something,' he muttered to himself. Probably get myself shot the very first day, he thought, Devane was the product of a French father and an Irish mother. Both of them dead when he was but twenty. Since then he had been to sea, tried his hand at farming when he had married a young new fiery Irish immigrant. They had fought constantly and he had left her after a year. He had signed the divorce papers two years ago after he'd come back from prospecting in the Rockies. The last two years he had done quite well as a detective. Had regular work with the wealthy in and around the Chesapeake area, and built up a reputation for getting results. If only he had that band of Mexican bandits, he could ride down in to that hell hole and get Buckland out, that is, if he was in there.

Getting up, Devane went to mount his horse and rode back a different way to town. If Kingsley had contacted the warden, Buckland might be on other work, he thought. He should be here soon then he could decide what they should do. He must not raise suspicion. To all intents and purposes, he was a prospector. Later in the evening he went to sit in a saloon. Watching people was part of his job. He had spent a lot of time guessing just who and what people might be. He watched to see if anyone was taking more than a passing interest in him. Mondell might have a man out here. As far as he knew Mondell did not know him. He had never worked for the Mondells. He had on more than one occasion seen the strutting egotist. He also had heard of his uncle's hard and unyielding way as a judge.

The following day he hung about waiting to see if Kingsley had arrived. He would see his name in the register as Carruthers. He often used a pseudo name when off on jobs. He should have had the letter from Benedict at least a week ago. Kingsley did not show up by noon so he took himself off riding north and then along the Gila River. There were good places to hide in the swampy parts. Then there was wild arid country. The terrain rose over a pass to the east. To the south and south-east was desert. The Colorado River ran down to the California Gulf. That might be the way to go if he could get Buckland out. Some sort of a diversion would be best. Buckland would have to know. If Kingsley could bribe the warden, something could be worked out. Again he spent the evening in the saloon which was full of rough looking men. Some were guards from the prison, and a few soldiers. Yuma was a place he didn't care for.

The next day Kingsley showed up. He came from the ferry on a buckboard with a couple of farmers. After he had checked into his room, he came down into the small lounge area and asked for coffee. When he came out to the street some fifteen minutes later, Devane bumped into him near the barber's shop. He said, 'Sorry! I'm Carruthers, my room number is six. I'll see you there in one hour.' Then walked off.

After he and Kingsley had a good talk in his room, Devane said he would go and take another look in the morning to see if he could spot Buckland. His father had given him a picture of him and he had studied it carefully. 'You go and see the sheriff, ask if he can talk with the warden about a visit. He will open any letter you try to give to Jonas,' Devane told Kingsley, who was using the name young Benedict had assumed. Kingsley was worried that Mondell might come out and disclose who Buckland really was and demand he be transported back to Baltimore.

'I think he won't do that. Mondell wants to kill him. He is obsessed, so I hear, with avenging his brother's death. He wishes to do it personally.'

The sun was gone down when Devane slipped along to Kingsley's room that evening. 'I've seen him. He was there today, and he was sticking close to a tall man like himself. He might be a Mexican as there were a few more bunched together. It would take a few men to get anyone out of there. The only way, I think, would be while they were on their way to the rock pit. There are plenty of guards, some on horse back, and all armed to the teeth.'

Kingsley looked glum. This was all out of his line. 'I saw the sheriff. He said he would try to see the warden. Pike is his name. He comes into town for a drink most evenings. He said if I offered him a sum of money, he was sure Pike would let me see John...Jonas for a few minutes to give him tobacco and soap. He suggested iodine and a bottle of brandy.'

'The guards will take the tobacco and brandy, you can bet on that, if Pike doesn't,' Devane opined.

'I told Sheriff Baker that I had already made a written request. He said that was good. He also said he had no jurisdiction over the prison, only if any of them escaped.'

Devane poured a large whiskey and handed it to Kingsley. 'I'll try to think of something. If you do see Buckland, ask him if he wants me to try to get him out? He has about ten months to go now. Perhaps he can hold on. I can come back next year. See he gets away some place.'

Kingsley agreed, and Devane took himself off to the saloon after he had eaten. This time, he thought, I've bitten off more than I can chew. He didn't wish to get himself killed trying to rescue Buckland.

Much as the challenge tempted him. Even if he did get him free, the guards and a posse would be on their trail in no time. Probably the soldiers too. They looked bored, he thought, as a few of them sat playing dominoes.

Back in the dark cell, Hawk leaned over and spoke to Buckland. 'Do you think someone is trying to get in touch with one of the prisoners?' he asked. He had seen the reflection during the afternoon and nudged Buckland. 'I think it is someone with a spyglass.'

'I don't know Hawk, I can't see any way to make a breakout. The guards would shoot right away. The men on horseback must have been sleeping, if there was someone up there,' he replied dejectedly. 'The best thing is to keep Collins on our side. My money is nearly gone. He might not help if he gets nothing.'

Hawk sighed. 'We must try to hold on, amigo!'

'How the hell can we survive on the slop they feed us? I'm already covered in sores and lice. I think I shall go stark raving mad. They treat us worse than animals. I don't know how you have kept your sanity all this time, Hawk,' he said bitterly.

Two days later, Collins came to tell Buckland he had a visitor coming on Sunday. Buckland just stood there flabberghasted. 'I don't believe it! There must be a mistake!' he gasped.

'Nope! Your uncle, Pike says. You be sure to ask for dough. I can get fruit and soap and such for you, and smokes.'

After Collins had moved on, Buckland turned to Hawk. 'Do you think he is razzing me?'

'If it was Drago I'd say yes. I think Collins was serious. Have you got an uncle?' Hawk asked giving Jonas a hard look.

Buckland went silent. 'Yes, I have,' he said a moment or two later after he had given it some thought. It was hardly likely his mother's brother would be coming out here, he was not a well man. His father had two sisters, so who could it be? His father must have arranged something. Doc Hughes must have sent his letter off to

Kingsley. That was it, it must be Kingsley, his godfather.

On Sunday, Jonas waited with apprehension for the visitors to arrive. There were not many. The usual tribe of girls came mincing in. Then he saw Marcus Kingsley looking just as apprehensive as he felt. He was a somewhat dapper man of five feet nine, about fifty years old with grey hair. His complexion showed he did not spend too much time out in the sun. His hands were whitish and well manicured. He looked at his godson with a gasp of horror. 'My God! What have they done to you? You look as if they tortured you, and starved you!'

Collins was not far away from them as Jonas took Kingsley to a bench in the shade near the stockade wall.

'I guess you got the doctor's letter,' he said.

'I did. Thank goodness or we would not have known where you were. Your father is most upset. He wrote me to try and get you out,' Kingsley whispered.

'There's no way to get out. Even if there

were, the guards would be after us in a flash. There's desert and the rivers, and wild country everywhere. Anyone who ever got out perished in the desert. Besides, I am too weak to run. It is all I can do to wield the sledge hammer in the pits. Someone ought to do something about the conditions here. The warden and the guards don't care. Nor does the doctor who is supposed to look after us. He is drunk most of the time,' Buckland said despairingly.

Kingsley passed over the parcel that he had brought and which had been thoroughly searched as he came in.

'There's some clean underwear and a bottle of iodine and some soap and ointment. The sheriff told me what they would let you have. There's a few cigars left. The guards took most. Here, take this money, hide it. I expect one of the guards will get you fruit and so forth. I hear the food is dreadful.'

Buckland slid the money down inside his pants. 'I'm obliged. There is one guard who takes care of Hawk and I. Hawk is a

Mexican and a friend. If I did get out I want him to get out too. He's been here for months now and has over a year to go yet, for stealing a chicken.'

Kingsley looked upset. 'There is a man here your father has sent. He could try to get you out but he says it looks impossible. I see they have a Gatling gun up on the stockade. I think it looks impossible.' Kingsley wiped the sweat off his face.

'Tell him not to try, I don't want another death on my conscience,' Buckland told Kingsley. 'I'm glad you came. I feel better now I know Dad knows where I am. Tell him not to worry. Somehow I'll survive.'

Collins got up from where he sat and came over. 'Time to go sir,' he told Kingsley.

Kingsley gave Buckland an awkward pat on his shoulder. 'Try to bear up,' he said and followed Collins.

After Kingsley had gone, Buckland went in search of Hawk who was shaping a new hat from some cactus fronds brought in by one of the girls who was busy with the three Mexican men. 'We have some smokes.' He gave a cigar to Hawk. 'And iodine, soap and fresh underwear, you can have a pair. He tossed some short pants to Hawk who looked delighted. His crotch was rubbed sore from the prison issue trousers.

Collins came back to join them looking pleased. 'Say, Buckland, your uncle is OK. He gave me twenty bucks and a bottle of brandy. You can have a swig later,' he winked. 'Listen, I gotta give you a few whacks now and then so's Drago and his pals don't think I've gone soft. I'll share a bottle with them when we go to town.'

'It's all right, Collins. We understand!' Buckland smiled. 'Just make sure you get us some fresh fruit and anything else you can.'

The following day Marcus Kingsley left town and went back across the river. The railroad still being constructed to El Centro, he took a coach there.

Devane also making ready to depart was down in the foyer when the well dressed man walked in. He turned away quickly as he recognized Louis Mondell. He saw that Mondell was taking his time registering and seemed to be taking note of the names on the last few pages. It came to Devane then that Mondell could pick off Buckland as he worked in the rock pit, if he were to place himself on the ridge where he had observed the prisoners from. He would be a crack shot most likely and could afford a good high-powered rifle. Quickly he went upstairs to collect his things and revise his plans.

SIX

Walking round to a back street, Devane went into the rooming-house he'd discovered earlier. He enquired of the dark complexioned man with heavy sideburns if he had a vacancy. The man gave him an appraising glare and asked how long he would be wanting the room for.

'Perhaps a couple of days,' Devane

told him and said he would be wanting breakfast and dinner. He was shown to a small room upstairs which looked a lot more cosy than the hotel room had been. He paid for two nights, left his bag and went round to the saloon he favoured.

Mondell freshened himself up and then went down to the street. He also headed for the saloon. He had discovered that these drinking places in the west were a mine of information if one got into conversation with the locals, and especially old timers who would talk their heads off for a pint or two. He asked for beer and some bread and cheese and then went to a table close to the window where some men sat nearby playing cards. He guessed they were prison guards as they seemed to be dressed in similar navy blue garb and wore gunbelts. Both men looked rather formidable, heavy set, and one had a scar beneath his left eye. A sardonic smile played about Mondell's lips at the thought of John Benedict being in their charge. They were discussing how they had tamed one of the renegades by putting him in the hell hole. Perhaps he need not bother about Buckland. A year at Yuma might well finish him.

Mondell sat eating his bread and cheese and sipping his beer thinking on what he should do. First he must discover if this Buckland really was John Benedict. Then he would try to see the warden and ask him to let him know when Buckland would be let out next year. The warden would no doubt be willing to divulge it for a price; send him word when he knew.

Devane sat at the rear next to the piano where he could observe Mondell and not be seen. Mondell was really obsessed he thought. His uncle, Judge Mondell, was a mean uncharitable bastard. No wonder Benedict had run off. I reckon he has come to make sure it is Benedict in that prison. I wonder how he found out? He'll say nothing about it, just wait till next year then kill him when he comes out, or, if that doesn't work out he'll have him followed and arrested. Might put a bounty hunter on to him.

Devane was worried. Perhaps he should

make a try to get Buckland out. He'd mentioned though to Kingsley there was a Mexican as well he wanted out, if it were possible.

Mondell finished his snack and got up and left the saloon. Devane followed and stood in the doorway and saw that he turned in at the livery stable. He walked down the street and stood where he could observe the stable. Ten minutes later Mondell rode out on a large horse that he could see was itching to go.

Walt Burgess was tamping down his pipe when Devane strolled up. 'Howdy,' he said. 'Thought you was leaving town?'

'I changed my mind, is the dun available?'

'Sure is! Jest had another easterner, he took Big Red. Sure hope he knows what he's doing.'

Devane laughed. 'If Red doesn't show up in the next ten minutes, I wouldn't worry.'

Burgess saddled the dun and brought him out. Devane mounted. 'Where did the greenhorn go?' he asked.

'Said he was a newspaper reporter. He wanted to get a look at the prisoners in the rock pit. Them guards sees him, they'll take a pot shot at him.'

'I guess he wants to write up a lot of stuff for the folks back east, so they can get a thrill out of it or get all riled up.' Devane laughed.

'Reckon they's a mighty peculiar lot them eastern folks, meaning no disrespect, Mister Carruthers.'

Devane chuckled and loped steadily off in the direction Mondell had taken. He headed towards the ridge from where he had watched the rock pit. I bet he's trying to make sure it is Benedict. Just how did he find out about him? I'm sure no one followed me. I took plenty of precautions. He could have traced him to Matarosa. Maybe someone spotted him there.

When Mondell reached the rim above the canyon he lay flat close to a bush. He pulled a spy glass from his pocket and began searching the rock pit.

Devane who was at the foot of the ridge behind some mesquite could see Mondell through his field glasses. He smiled when he saw Mondell's horse tied alongside some bushes a hundred yards away. He reined his horse over and dismounted. 'Hey, Big Red! How're doing?' he said. The horses rubbed muzzles and exchanged some horse talk. Devane untied the big horse and led him away with the dun.

As Mondell lay watching the prisoners down below hammering away at the rocks, he chuckled. That ought to cut that strutting arrogant Benedict down to size. Where the hell is he? At the far end where the canyon narrowed and where it was blocked off with thirty feet of barbed wire and coils both sides of it, he saw a few men with picks some yards up the sloping bank. He focused on two tall men. One had on a straw hat with fronds sticking out for a brim. The other wore an old round crowned, rangeman's hat. The two men suddenly stopped what they were doing, removed their hats and mopped their brows with their sleeves. He stiffened. Yes, it was Benedict, he was sure. He looked lean and dishevelled. It'll kill him. Mondell chuckled again. A guard came across and seemed to be telling them to get back to work.

There was a sound along the rim and Mondell put his spy glass into his pocket and slid downwards when he saw the horse coming. The rider had a rifle slung across his back. It must be a guard. Very quickly he went down the slope using the cover of rocks and small bush. When he got to the place he had left the horse he looked around in dismay. Big Red was gone. 'Damn it,' he swore. He was sure he had tied it up tightly. Sweat broke out on his brow. What if a guard had taken it?

'You looking for your horse?' a voice hailed him over to his left.

Mondell swung round. A rider was coming towards him leading his mount. He did not look like a guard, he observed with relief.

'Yes, he must have got loose,' Mondell replied.

'You'd better get mounted,' Devane gave Mondell a brief smile. 'It isn't safe to ride around here. There're prisoners just over the ridge and guards on horseback with rifles.'

Just as Mondell mounted, his face red, the spy glass dropped from his pocket. The horse jumped as it clattered to the ground. Mondell yanked its head in tight in annoyance at himself.

Devane got down and retrieved the glass and handed it up to Mondell. 'I hope it isn't broken,' he said evenly and got back on to his horse. 'Well, I'm heading back for town, you coming?'

'Yes, of course,' Mondell called.

When they came to the livery stable Burgess came out to take the horses from them. 'I see you two met up then. Red give you any trouble?' he asked giving Mondell a raking stare.

'No, he went well enough,' he said and handed over two dollars. He waited for Devane. He was still wondering how he just happened to be around when the horse got loose, if it did. 'You staying in Yuma?' he said casually, regarding him closely.

'I've been prospecting. Haven't found anything though. I'll be moving on in a

100

day or two,' Devane said affably. 'Will you be staying long? I understand you're a newspaper man. Looking for something special to excite the readers?'

Mondell's eyes narrowed slightly. 'I was most interested to find out about the prisoners here. They say it is a hell of a place to be landed in.'

'I wouldn't like to be incarcerated up on that hill, nor work in that hell pit,' Devane replied.

'Do you know if anyone ever escapes?'

'I doubt it. They wouldn't get far, there's miles of desert to the south and east and it's pretty wild any way you go. The guards would soon catch them.'

'I expect they are mostly killers, rapists and robbers,' Mondell said scathingly. 'I was wondering if the warden would give me an interview.'

'Best thing would be to ask the sheriff. He would know. I wouldn't waste your sympathy on those scum though, if I were you,' Devane said looking Mondell squarely in the eyes.

'Ah, yes! The sheriff! Well thank you

for finding my horse, Mister...' Mondell smiled back.

'Carruthers,' Devane said. 'I wish you luck,' he added and walked off. He went to his room and slept till it was supper time. The meal was surprisingly good and cooked by the man's wife. It was good wholesome home cooking, the kind Devane had not come across for some time. Later he went to the saloon and played poker for over an hour with some locals. He lost twenty dollars and figured the two who won it needed it more than he did. The Benedicts had plenty of money. He could have used a lot more than he had so far. He would not put in for much in expenses like some did. He valued John Benedict as a client, he had given him plenty to work with. It looked as if he would be on his way back home soon though. It all depended on Mondell. He must stay here till he left Yuma.

The subject of his thought walked in just then and went to stand at the bar. The saloon was almost full. Some rangemen were talking loudly. If Mondell were a true writer he would be seated somewhere with a notebook and pencil, taking down what he saw. There was plenty of colour here. Soldiers, prison guards and owl hoots, drifters and all kinds. Enough to fill a book.

Mondell remained at the bar, a glass of brandy in his hand which was on the raw side. His stomach had not been too good, so he felt it would kill any bug he might have picked up from eating the atrocious food he had been forced to consume of late. The only consoling factor was that Benedict alias Buckland would be eating far worse slop, and suffering indescribable privations. The sheriff had told him it was mostly unbearably hot from May to November. He had also promised him, for a hundred dollars, that he would write and let him know the date of Buckland's release next August. Tomorrow he would be on his way out of this appalling place.

The group of drifters were becoming raucous at the bar. One of them turned to Mondell. 'What are you drinking, Mister?'

Mondell gave him a cursory glance.

'Brandy!' he said and finished his drink then turned to leave.

'Hey, Mister!' another one called. 'You want a shot of red-eye?' His companions sniggered.

'Thank you, no.' Mondell replied sharply.

'What's the matter? Ain't we good enough for you eastern dudes?' The first one asked.

Looking decidedly annoyed Mondell tried again to leave. 'I really don't care to drink any more,' he said.

'Told you we ain't good enough to drink with, Bud,' a younger one of the group of five men, put in. 'Stuck up sod, he is!'

Pushing his way towards the exit, Mondell, holding down his anger, brushed past Clive Bodine, a top hand from a ranch some miles north of Yuma, and he swung round and reached for Mondell. 'Why don't you look where yer going?' he snapped.

Mondell turned. 'It is you who should be looking where you are going, clumsy oaf!'

Bodine stood swaying a moment then he let fly and caught Mondell a blow to the side of the head and he staggered and was hit in the back by the batwing door which propelled him right into Bodine who, in turn, stepped on the foot of one of the drifters. Having already had a lot to drink, he flung himself at Mondell again after someone had pushed him forward.

Mondell managed to extricate himself. He was furious at being the butt of amusement of these rough men. A voice from somewhere amongst the midst of them called. 'What are you waiting for, dude? You yeller?'

Devane had got up to watch and was waiting to see if a fight was in the offing. He was thinking it would have done no harm for Mondell to have taken a drink. It was probably his first experience of this western lifestyle.

Mondell was still trying to make for the exit when Bodine clutched at him again. 'Don't you turn your back on me you bull-shit Yankee. I ain't finished with you yet!'

This was too much, Mondell lost his cool. Although he looked something of a lightweight, he was in fact lean and sinewy, and kept himself fit. He flung a fist at Bodine's jaw, taking him by surprise and he went staggering against a table knocking all the glasses and a bottle to the floor. The place was in an uproar. Two cowpunchers called to Bodine to whup the easterner.

Looking rather embarrassed, Mondell pulled at his broadcloth coat which was now splattered with beer stains. He parried Bodine's next attempt. From the corner of his eye he caught sight of the man who had been out riding, Carruthers, that was his name. I'll show them damn it, that I'm no coward. He went after Bodine who was prancing about with his fists up.

'Come on Clive, show the dude!' A voice shouted from the rear.

Mondell hit Bodine a short jab on the jaw as he came in. Then Bodine swung and caught him with a lucky blow to the side of his neck. They broke apart eyeing each other. Mondell waited. He wished he had his coat off. He thought of the blow that had killed his brother. He did not wish to fight this drunken man. He could not get out of it. He did not wish to be called yellow.

Bodine rushed in and Mondell stepped aside and let him fall into the throng of excited men who had begun to see the easterner was no pushover. It irked Bodine that he couldn't finish off this lighter man. He began to circle now more in possession of his faculties. They exchanged a few ineffective blows. Then Mondell saw his chance and gave Bodine a few nasty blows to the ribs, then with one clean upper-cut, he laid him out.

The place went quiet for some seconds, then there was a lot of chattering, some subdued exchanges of opinions. In general the drifters and locals were quite shaken that the easterner had beaten Bodine, a quite large solid man, and who was known for his violent and mean temper when he was on a drinking bout.

Mondell did not stay for anyone to congratulate him, and there were a few who would have been glad to shake his hand for laying out Bodine. He went out to the street from the permeated foul smelling saloon and breathed in the cool freshness of the evening. As he walked up the street a girl suddenly stepped out from the shadows. 'Señor, you like buy Chaquita tequila?' she asked.

In no doubt what the girl was really after, Mondell stood thinking a moment. She was quite pretty, he thought. He glanced up the street where two men were mounting their horses. He could see no one else. 'Why not,' he said, as she smiled at him. She led him by the hand into another darkened street till they came to an adobe house. The kitchen smelled of chilli peppers as she guided him into the bedroom through a curtained doorway. There was little but the small bed and a couple of chairs. She drew the curtains over the glassless window through which came the smells of the desertland and the river.

The girl poured some tequila into a glass for Mondell as he began to undress. 'Nobody ever beat Señor Bodine before,' she said.

'I did not wish to fight him,' Mondell

told her and drank down the fiery liquid and coughed. The fight had got his adrenalin flowing, the girl had an attractive, seductive figure, her breasts young and lifted. He reached for her in a hurry. Already he had forgotten the fight. He used her vigorously until she cried out to him to stop, wrestling with him.

SEVEN

The sun was up and the day bright when Mondell awoke. He lay a while to gather his mind together. He got up slowly, his head throbbing as he opened the door to pull in the jug of supposedly hot water. He shaved with difficulty telling himself how glad he would be to get on that train and leave this worst of all places. He smiled thinly as he wondered how Bodine would be feeling. At West Point he had taken instruction in boxing, fencing and weaponry. All of this had served him well.

It was gone nine o'clock when he ordered his breakfast in the small dining-room. He said just coffee and toast. The Mexican woman brought him some thick pieces of bread, jam and butter and a pot of coffee. He shrugged resignedly.

The train was due out at 12.30 so he decided to go and buy his ticket and then finish packing his bag. He was half way along the street when Bodine came out from an alleyway. His face looked bruised, and an eye was puffed and had a black ring around it. The street was quite busy with pedestrians and wagons and horses.

'Hey, you, easterner!' Bodine called to Mondell. 'I'm calling you! You hear me?'

Mondell stopped walking as Bodine stepped into the street. His mind went back to the things he had read about gun fights and the way these western people sometimes settled their differences. Surely this idiot was not challenging him to a duel?

'Bodine!' he called as one or two people stopped on the sidewalk; some slipped into shop doorways. 'I fought you last evening,

110

It is over, finished!'

'No it ain't. You hurt my girl. For that I'm going to kill you.' Bodine shouted at him.

The man was obsessed, Mondell thought. Surely that little whore couldn't be his girl. She was anybody's who chose to pay for her. The bitch must have told him.

'Listen, Bodine. I have no gun, and I don't intend going to jail for killing you over some whore.'

A bullet hit the signpost over a shop doorway a few feet from Mondell. He jumped. Then he heard another voice along the boardwalk.

Sheriff Baker had come out of a cafe. 'Bodine, you put that gun away and get on back to the ranch.'

'Sheriff, you keep outta this. I'm going to kill that son-of-a-bitch. He hurt Chaquita bad and I'm calling him.'

'He's mad!' Mondell called to the sheriff. 'I had to fight him last evening and I didn't wish to.'

Baker drew his revolver and came on up the street and passed Mondell. 'I'll put him in jail till you've left town,' he said from the corner of his mouth.

'Keep back Baker, I mean it. I'll shoot you too if you come any closer. The dude can buckle on a gun belt. I gotta right to call him. He hurt my girl!'

'Chaquita isn't your girl, Clive. Now put up that gun and come peaceable.'

A bullet kicked up dust only inches from Baker's feet. He stopped walking and Mondell went to him. 'I'm not going to jail for killing that fool over a whore,' he said stridently.

Baker gave him a look. 'If you did kill him you wouldn't have to go to jail. It would be self defence!'

'It's your job, Sheriff to stop him. I don't want to fight him. I have no gun.'

Suddenly there was a thump and a pistol landed in front of Mondell in the dust. A cold hard voice told him to pick it up.

Mondell could not believe it. Surely he was still in bed and dreaming. Once again he was being goaded into a fight. This time he might be killed.

Something of a crowd had now gathered

along the street. Everyone was waiting expectantly. What would the easterner do?

'I'm waiting,' Bodine called.

Chuck Norton, Bodine's buddy, shouted at Mondell. 'Pick the gun up, you been called, dude. You, Sheriff keep out of it. I got a rifle lined on your back.'

Baker walked to the side as he felt a prod in his back. He got on to the boardwalk, as he was told.

Sweat was running down Mondell's nose. He thought of the lectures he had had from an old sergeant who had spent time out here fighting Indians. He picked up the pistol slowly and spun the cylinder. The handle was a nicely honed piece of walnut. There was one empty chamber, he spun it past the hammer. Then he lifted his hat and gave a quick glance to see where the sun was. The fact he had no holster seemed not to worry Bodine. No doubt he felt so sure of himself the slight edge didn't worry him. Was he that good?

This time Bodine's voice was impatient as he called once again. 'Let's get on with it. I ain't got all day.'

Mondell smiled briefly. Perhaps Bodine had but only a few more minutes. Of course he might be the unlucky one. He felt angry as he walked onwards and moved sideways into some shade. Bodine also moved and came onwards, his hand flexing at his side. Suddenly he went into a crouch and Mondell, whose eyes had been fixed on that hand, turned sideways on as his right arm swung up, his thumb pulling back the hammer, his finger squeezing off a shot.

There was a loud gasp from the crowd as they saw Bodine's gun fire, the bullet hitting the dust inches from Mondell's back foot, then a second ploughed into the ground a few feet in front of Mondell. Bodine was already falling forward, the second bullet from Mondell's pistol having landed an inch from the first which had landed in his heart. Bodine hit the ground hard and lay face down.

Mondell was shaking as he dropped the gun and walked away stiff backed. Any minute he expected a bullet to hit him. He had no idea how many of those

114

who watched might be friends of Bodine. There was the one who had loaned him the revolver.

As the first shot was fired, Baker had swung round fast and taken the rifle from Norton. Now he walked to Bodine and turned him over on his back. He was quite dead.

Norton had sunk down and sat on the boardwalk in a stupor. He had never doubted Bodine would kill the easterner. He was shattered. People everywhere were discussing the swiftness of Mondell's arm, and the way he'd stood sideways and leaned back as he fired.

Baker sent someone to fetch the undertaker. Something about Mondell gave him the shivers. He would be glad to see him on to the train in just an hour. The Mex girl was covered in bruises, her sister had told him she had been frightened badly by Mondell.

Devane, who had witnessed the whole scene, was also shaken. While it was true Mondell had been given little choice but to fight, he had been an unknown entity. Bodine had been too confident in himself. It just went to show, one could never be sure of anything. One good thing, however, was that Mondell was leaving today. He had no intention of killing Buckland until he came out of prison, and with his skill with guns would be quite a formidable foe. Mondell might even have the gall to call out Buckland after he was let out of prison. He could kill him and walk away free. As he walked off to fetch his bags, Devane thought also about the Mexican girl. What the hell kind of man was Mondell to have used her so? It would seem John Benedict would have done the world a service had he killed Louis instead of Roger, he thought. He was glad he now had more knowledge of Mondell, though. It would be invaluable when he came back next year to get Buckland away safely, and he was sure that he would be doing just that after he had reported back.

Baker was at the station to see Mondell off. He had a bottle of whiskey and

116

some ham sandwiches with him. He felt exhausted. It had been exciting though. His theory had worked. He had actually enjoyed killing Bodine, the loud mouthed fool. If only it had been John Benedict. How marvellous that would have been. The train got underway and he sat back with relief.

Paul Devane slipped on to the last passenger carriage as the train pulled out. He had decided he would get off at Tucson and go to Tombstone for a little relaxation. He had heard much about this place. Unlike Mondell, Devane liked the west. When he was done with this assignment next year, he would stay in the west. Perhaps Denver would be a good place to put down his roots. At thirty he ought to be thinking about it. The train rumbled on and he sat back, pulled his hat over his face and went to sleep.

EIGHT

Thanks to Marcus Kingsley having greased Pike's palm, life for Collins was somewhat easier, in that he also slipped Pike the odd stogey after Buckland had given him money to buy things. Pike had kept other guards such as Drago off his back, those who had not liked Collins being made a guard before his sentence was finished. Money sure had its influences, Collins thought as he walked across the yard to join Buckland who was hunkered down by the stockade wall. Soon he would be leaving this place and starting out in the real world. At thirty-eight, it would be hard getting a job. Well he still had plenty of work left in him. He would head for Denver and try his luck there.

Buckland greeted him as he sat down beside him. 'I guess you must be looking forward to getting your official release,

Collins,' he said rather tiredly. If it hadn't been for Collins, he was sure he would have been dead by now. Then there was Hawk. He had helped him keep his sanity. He watched Hawk as he limped over to join some of the Mexicans.

'Yep, I can't wait to get gone from here,' Collins responded and handed Jonas a cigar. 'You'll be leaving soon as well. I reckon you must be thinking about it; where you'll be off to. You'll need plenty of rest for a while, some good food down you.'

Buckland smiled half heartedly. 'My head feels so woolly lately, I can't think at all. I don't care where I go really as long as it is well away from here.'

Collins gave him a thoughtful look. 'Won't you be seeing your uncle? I'd have thought a gent like you would have a family somewhere. A good home to go to.'

Getting up, Buckland ignored the probing remarks. 'Is there some way we could help Hawk? He won't last another six months in here'

'I don't see how. Pike don't like the Mexicans much. Once you're gone, Hawk won't be so protected.'

'What if Pike were offered money? Would he let him be a guard as he did you?'

'Never! Drago and Co wouldn't go for that. Pike might do something though if he was offered plenty of cash. He'd want to have it in his hands first.'

'Could you get permission for me to go and talk with him?'

Collins sat thinking a while. 'It ain't easy to see him. If I get a chance I'll try and ask him.' He got up as he saw Drago and Bull having words across the square and walked away.

It was two days later that Collins came for Buckland after he had been locked up for the night. 'Come with me and be careful what you say to Pike,' he said. 'He's been drinking and he can get real mean.'

Pike sat behind a desk in his small office which was lighted by two lamps. 'You get out Collins. I'll send for you when I want you,' he snarled, blowing cigar smoke into Buckland's face.

Buckland stood stiffly, looking into the bloodshot eyes of his custodian. He would not let him see he was the least afraid of him. Pike would despise weakness.

'All right, Buckland. What's your beef?'

'No beef, sir. I was wondering if you knew the date of my release?'

'You came here to ask me that?' Pike was astounded.

'Not exactly, but it would be nice to know there won't be a hitch. I have reason to believe there may be someone waiting when I go out...someone who wishes me harm. So help me, I never took that bank money. I believe the deputy knows well enough about that. It would be helpful if I could go before it gets daylight. I could make it worth your while,' Buckland ventured.

Pike's eyes narrowed. 'When you go out of here Buckland, you are on your own. I'll be glad to see the back of you. Someone's been complaining about conditions here, and I don't like that,' he spat out.

'I know nothing of that. It couldn't have been from me. I know you have a difficult job here. What I really wanted to ask was if there is something you might do to help Fernandez. All he did was steal one lousy chicken because he was hungry, and got two years. The soldiers did much worse that that in the war!'

'Buckland, you got a damned nerve. What's that lousy greaser to you, eh?'

'He has helped me keep my sanity in this hell hole, and I believe he will die soon if he is not let out. I mean it about the money. I can get money when I get out, but it may take a little while.'

Pike took a long swig from his glass of whiskey. He was thinking hard. Who the hell would care about the Mex if he disappeared? 'Just how much did you have in mind? Why should I trust you, Buckland?'

Feeling he was getting somewhere with Pike, Buckland ran his tongue round a dry mouth. 'If I give my word I will keep it. You will have to help keep me alive though. Let me out earlier than usual. As soon as I can I will have money sent to a bank for you wherever you say. What would you want for the favour?'

It was Pike's turn to run his tongue around his lips. His face was expressionless now. He'd be good at poker, Buckland was thinking. 'What about one thousand dollars? It's a big favour you're asking. I could lose my job.' Pike took another drink. He was thinking that he could quit the prison job and buy a nice little piece of land someplace for that much money. He had saved a little. This was his chance to leave the hell hole. 'Send it to the National Bank at Phoenix and let me know when it is there. I'll have to think about this first though.'

Buckland gave a shudder of relief. 'One thousand to Phoenix. I'll send a letter to you saying. "Have arrived Phoenix. Will be in touch. Jack". How would that be? As I've said, it will take two or three weeks to arrange it.'

Pike got up and strode to the door, opened it and yelled for Collins. 'Get this fool out of here,' he barked. As Buckland went out of the door, he whispered to him. 'August 21st, you'll be out of here.'

As they walked back to the cell, Collins gave Buckland a strange look. 'It ain't usual for Pike to give more than five minutes. What the hell was you two talking about in there?'

'Better you don't know, Collins,' said Buckland. The 21st of August was still ringing in his ear. He felt weak, dizzy. Only three more weeks. And if Pike did as he asked, perhaps Hawk would be free too. How he would like to spend time with him away from this place. He was a friend he did not wish to let go of.

Warden Pike was very suspicious of Sheriff Baker's visit. Buckland again. Just who the hell was he that so many people were interested in his release? Must be some important person. Politics, that's it. Same with the Mex. He was educated, so Collins said, and Buckland wanted him out. Should have asked for more dinero. He ain't getting his gold watch back nor his good suit. I gotta see he don't get killed. Collins can help. We can say the greaser croaked. I'll have that geezer outta here tonight. Baker thinks it's the 22nd that Buckland gets out, that should keep him out of the way. Can't figure what he's at.

Paul Devane was not surprised when he got the note from John Benedict. He had purposely kept himself free the last few weeks. This time he would go via Denver and then down to Las Cruces and on to Benson.

After he had picked up $3,000 and some expense money, his fee placed in his bank account, Devane packed his bag and got on the way. Rumour had it that the constabulary were no longer interested in young John Benedict as witnesses of the supposed murder were not now ready to come forward. It was just an accident they were now saying, those young fools who'd been Roger Mondell's friends. Still he could not advise young John Benedict to go back to Baltimore until it was official. The first thing he must do was get

125

Jonas Buckland away to safety. For certain Mondell would be coming, or sending someone to do his dirty work. He would hardly be welcome in Yuma. Baker would watch him like a hawk, if he clapped eyes on him.

Louis Mondell smiled after reading the scrawled letter from Baker. So, August 22nd was the date of Buckland's release. He seldom now thought of him as John Benedict. Fourteen days to go. He would be on his way soon. A week to check things out. This time he would need help he thought. Someone he could use to go into Yuma and find out a few things for him.

Mondell was like a caged panther as he made his preparations for travel. He had bought a long range hunting rifle. He would take his Colt though, he still wanted to look into the eyes of Roger's killer when he did it. However, if that became impossible the rifle would be the answer. After it was done he would go home and marry Madeliene Holsteader. The Holsteaders were extremely rich. Now he was in partnership with his father, it would be a desirable alliance.

Buckland was counting the days, hoping Pike would not let him down. Collins would be gone on Friday and the following Wednesday he would walk out of those gates. He had told Hawk about his talk with Pike. Hawk was sceptical. He was sure Pike would make it worse for him when Buckland was gone. He would have to try and get away somehow, even if he got shot it would be better than dying a slow death through starvation, and he was sure he was destined to do so very soon.

Collins was quite edgy of late. Going out looking for work would not be easy, especially if it were known of his stretch in Yuma. He greeted one of the guards in rather a surly manner when he came to tell him that Pike wished to see him. He began to sweat. What the hell did he want? He knocked at the office door.

Pike opened it after a few minutes. He liked to see the sweat on Collins' face. 'Come on in,' he said. 'I got a plan to get the greaser out. Tonight we'll do it. If you ever open your mouth about it, I'll see you never get out of here, you understand?'

Collins' mouth dropped open. He gulped hard. 'You know you can trust me. I never let you down,' he said rather feebly.

'You tell that 'breed to throw a fit when he has his grub tonight. You carry him to the morgue hut. Bates and you will take him out in a coffin before daylight and bury him. Well, not really. You think of something to get Bates out of the way while you let the 'breed out then you put the lid back on and fill in the hole.'

Collins was struck dumb. Pike sat waiting. He almost burst out laughing. 'Go on, get out and you'd better not bungle it, a lot rides on this. My job for one thing.'

When Collins came back in with the work party he was a bag of nerves. Everything depended on him. He had managed to get Hawk alone at noon. Hawk had looked at him with disdain. 'I don't believe this, it's a plot to get me shot.'

'No, I think your amigo had something to do with this. He seen Pike a while back. I reckon he must've promised him plenty of dough. I reckon he got plenty stashed some place. Just you do as I say and it will work. You want out don't you?'

'Yes, I want out. I'm half dead anyway. I don't care one way or the other now.' Fernandez shrugged. Inside he was shaking. Had Buckland really fixed it?

When he threw his fit during the evening meal, which was more bread and pig slop, Hawk suddenly let out a horrible sound. Then he rolled on the ground holding his stomach, pulling up his knees. Buckland knelt down beside him full of concern. Hawk winked then a guard came up and kicked him hard in his back, and he let out a yell.

Collins who had been prowling about came rushing across. 'He's in a fit! Here, you!' he called to a new youngish prisoner, 'Get hold of his legs we'll take him to the sick hut.' The startled prisoner did as he was told and he and Collins got Fernandez across to the sick hut, which was used as a mortuary as well. There were a few roughly made coffins at the rear of it. They put him down on a bunk next to an elderly man who was near to death's door. Collins covered him with a threadbare blanket. He bent over and whispered in Hawk's ear. 'I'll be back later, you stay quiet now like you was dying.'

It was still quite cold when Collins got Bates out of his bunk. 'The greaser croaked, we gotta get him buried, Pike says. No need to make a big fuss there's been too many deaths, and he wants it kept sorta quiet,' he told Bates, who was somewhat slow of comprehension.

The guard at the stockade gate grumbled loudly. Collins showed the note from Pike saying they were to be let out with the wagon. When they got to the cemetery where several crosses were either fallen down or leaning, they set to to dig the grave. The ground being rather hard it took some time to get down far enough to satisfy Collins. It was far short of the normal depth, but Bates was in no mood to argue. They lowered the coffin down and pulled out the ropes. At that moment Collins stood up straight listening. 'Ray, I hear an antelope or maybe a rabbit out there,' he pointed out towards some bushes. 'You got the rifle you go see what it is. We could have us a real nice meal tonight.'

Bates went to fetch the rifle from the wagon and went off in the direction Collins had indicated. Very quickly he ripped off the lid and spoke to Hawk.'Come on get out fast and take off,' he pulled him up by the arm. Feeling frozen and stiff, not to mention quite terrified, Fernandez let Collins help him up from the hole. He gave Collins a quick pat on the shoulder and thanked him emotionally, then he slid under the wagon, just as Bates came lumbering back, and crawled away for the bushes.

'I didn't see no animal. You must've heard a snake or something,' Bates told Collins.

Smiling to himself and rubbing the cold sweat from his neck, Collins climbed onto the wagon. 'Let's go,' he said, giving one last look at the mound of earth that was Fernandez's official resting place.

It was two days before word got around that Hawk had expired. Some just shrugged. Buckland had a hard time containing his excitement. Collins kept away from him till it had died down some. The Bedfords were in sombre mood. It had shaken them badly.

After he had slid along in the sand and bush, Hawk lay waiting till the wagon had gone out of sight. The sky was yellow to the east as he got up cautiously and put one foot in front of the other. The leg irons gone, he shuffled along in the poor old sandals. He wore a dead man's clothing. He didn't care. He was out, free. He wanted to yell it at the sky. In his hand was a paper bag, a chunk of bread and cheese inside it. Collins had also given him two dollars and an old sweat stained, wide brimmed hat. He headed westwards for the river stumbling along amongst the scrub bush. When he reached it he would go south and try to locate the Mexican whom Collins had once said kept goats and a few sheep, and ask him if he might lay up a few days. He would give him a dollar and help him with his chores after he'd had some rest. Then he would come back and watch out for Jonas on the Wednesday morning. He would have to be careful though, he thought. But he was dead wasn't he? Pike could hardly pull him in again, it would take some explaining. Perhaps Jonas would need help. He was in even worse a state than himself. It would be nice to thank him properly for arranging his escape, and he was sure he must have promised Pike plenty of dinero, or how else would he have got out.

His position was not good. All he had was the two dollars, and he must give one to the peon. To get work would not be easy. Just to get food would be a problem, he could not be caught stealing again. He remembered the bag in his hand and took out the bread and cheese and began to wolf it down. The sky behind him was already yellowing.

NINE

After getting off the train at Benson Devane left his bag at the station office then headed for the main street. It did not take long to discover Doctor Hughes's office. Inside a small room seated on a bench was a middle aged woman and a younger man. Nodding, Devane sat down on a straight backed chair and took out his watch and consulted it. The two locals gave him looks of idle curiosity.

Waiting patiently until a heavily pregnant young woman, and the two others, had gone, Devane got up as Hughes came out wiping his hands on a towel. 'You wish to see me?' he asked.

'If you can spare me a few minutes. I'm not ill, it is a personal matter,' Devane told him.

Looking rather puzzled, Hughes invited him into his inner sanctum where Devane got straight to the point. 'I believe you have a horse belonging to a Jonas Buckland, is that right?'

Hughes gave him a startled look then took his time before he answered. 'Who are you? What is it to you?'

'Does the name Marcus Kingsley mean any thing to you?' Devane asked avoiding the questions.

'It might,' said doc, still cautious.

'Jonas Buckland was sent to Yuma Prison a year ago. He will be coming out shortly and will need his horse. I am to take it to him. He cannot come here. I'm sure you understand why. I shall be seeing that he is safe when he does come out, that is all I can tell you.'

'I see,' said Hughes, thinking quickly. 'When do you want the horse?'

'As soon as I can get it. I would also like to purchase another one with gear and bedroll, if that is possible. A good solid one. I'll pay whatever is necessary, you understand.'

'All right! I know someone who deals in horses. It might take an hour or two.

135

Where shall I find you?'

'I'll be in the saloon over there. When you have them ready, just look in, don't say anything. I'll come to your office. Here is a hundred and fifty.' Devane gave doc the money.

Hughes took it quickly. He hoped he could trust this man. Kingsley must have sent him or how would he know of him? Mrs Allard would have to wait. What of the $1,000 he still had belonging to Buckland? He decided to think about it while he went after the horse.

Devane enjoyed his glass of beer and two ham and pickle sandwiches while he waited. His journey had been long and tedious, though he had stopped over in Denver. That was the place he would most likely settle in when he was through with this assignment. Folks in the west, he thought, were on the whole, honest to God, down to earth, except the lawless lot and they were phasing out considerably of late. A large man came in then arresting his thought. He wore a star on a leather vest and wore a low slung Colt at his hip. He

136

gave Devane a raking over with his eyes.

About an hour and a half later the good doctor poked his head over the batwings and looked around the room which had but a few occupants. Devane gave a slight nod.

'You looking for somebody, Doc?' Hatcher asked inquisitively, as he stood at the bar.

'Morning Jed,' Hughes said and disappeared.

Devane waited about five minutes before he got up and walked slowly out into the street. He sauntered across to look into the window of a saddlery. Then went onwards and slipped into doc's office.

Hughes was looking pleased with himself. To tell the truth he was glad the horse was going. Hatcher frequently came snooping around his paddock and that made him nervous. 'I got a good horse and what you wanted for eighty dollars.' He handed the change to Devane. 'I have both horses behind my house which is in the next street. We can go the back way.'

'Good!' Devane answered and followed

137

Hughes out through a back door and then up and across and to the rear of the neat little house. When he saw the horses and had a good look at the hoofs which were well shod, he smiled at Hughes. 'I'm much obliged for your trouble.'

Hughes was looking uneasy and fidgeting. 'I have some money that Buckland gave me. I've taken a hundred for feed for the horse. Here's nine hundred. I expect he will be needing it.' Doc took the folded money from his pocket and handed it over.

Devane looked at him then took the money, then he burst out laughing. 'By God, Doc! If only all the people were as honest as you, what a nice world it would be! Here, take this. Johnny would want you to have it for taking such good care of his horse.' Devane handed doc another hundred.

Reddening, Hughes was about to decline the offer then he thought of the new stethoscope he wanted to buy, and Megan's birthday was coming up soon. 'I never thought Jonas should have been arrested. It was all an unfortunate mistake,' he said.

'Yes, that it was,' said Devane. He got up into the saddle of Buckland's horse. 'So long, Doc. I'll give him your regards.'

'Please do. Tell him they never found the money.'

Taking a back way to the station, Devane picked up his bag and headed for Tucson. He would board the train with the horses from there.

Louis Mondell was just two days behind Devane. He too got off the train at Benson. First he booked himself into the hotel for one night. The heat was fierce and he was glad he had brought a lighter weight suit. It was in the late afternoon when he went into the sheriff's office where he found the deputy who sat behind Sheriff Riggs's desk. Hatcher was feeling irritated. This was the hottest summer that he could remember, since he had come to Benson. He was ready to quit. Riggs would never retire. There was little hope of his getting his job, as he could see. Folks had been none too friendly since the robbery. He was sure

139

some of them believed he had taken the money and hidden it. 'You looking for somebody?' he glared at Mondell, then he recognized him.

'Hello Hatcher! I see you're still here,' Mondell said coolly.

'Yep, I'm still here. I figure you'll be on your way to Yuma. Is there something I can do for you?' Hatcher asked eagerly as he wiped his face with his bandanna which needed a good wash.

'I have a room at the hotel. When you are off duty, or whatever, come and see me.'

Hatcher had jumped up. 'Sure, I'll come around six. Town's kinda quiet. The heat's getting to folks,' he said and watched Mondell go out into the street.

Hatcher was there on the dot of six, by his watch.

'Sit down, Hatcher,' Mondell told him in almost military fashion. He did not wish to be on familiar terms with this man whom he would not normally give the time of day to. He poured out a generous amount of whiskey into his tooth glass

140

and handed it to him. 'I'll put it plain,' Mondell started. 'I want to hire you to help me to do a job. Jonas Buckland is being released on the 22nd August. There are reasons I do not wish to go into Yuma. Well, last time I was there I shot a man. In self-defence, but he was a local. I feel the sheriff would not wish to see me there again.'

Hatcher grinned and licked his lips. 'I figured you and this Buckland was pals, last time you come asking about him.'

Mondell gave him a withering look. 'Buckland is no friend of mine. What I want you to do is go into Yuma and find out when they usually let out the ones being released. The time is important.'

'Is that all you want me to do?' Hatcher said, looking disappointed. 'I can't get off just like that. Riggs will ask questions if I want more than a day.'

'I'll pay you well enough. You can't make much as a deputy. What would you want for helping me, say, for a couple of weeks?'

A look of greed spread across Hatcher's

face. He sweated profusely having swallowed the good Kentucky bourbon down quickly. 'What's it worth to you?'

Mondell sensed Hatcher's greed. 'Say, two-hundred-and-fifty now and two-hundred-and-fifty more when the job is finished. I may want you to do other things.'

'Make it seven-hundred-and-fifty, my grub and the train fare for me and my hoss. Half before I leave. I have to give up my job and it ain't easy getting another.'

'All right! You get me a good horse and gear for camping. Here is two hundred. You get your ticket for the train tomorrow and meet me at the station,' Mondell said in a dismissive tone.

Hatcher got up. He went through the door in a hurry. Mondell gave him the creeps, but it was too good an offer to turn down. He had already been thinking of pulling his freight. Had mentioned it to Riggs, so he wouldn't be surprised.

Riggs wasn't at all surprised. In fact he was delighted. Hatcher, he thought, would be no loss.

When Devane saw the man who had just entered the cafe he stiffened. He had not quite seen the face as the man was tethering his horse. He searched his memory as to where he had seen him. It was Saturday and the streets were quite busy with wagons and pedestrians. Some prison guards were collecting rations from the store, most of which, Devane thought, would be used by the warden and guards, the remainder for the prisoners. Kingsley had written his associate John Benedict about the appalling conditions after his second visit just two months ago. Buckland would be in bad shape when he came out and hardly fit to travel. It had to be done though. Put a lot of miles between them and this hell hole.

Hatcher turned his head and gazed around the room. It came to Devane then. The deputy from Benson. He lowered his head. Now what the hell was he doing here? He was not wearing a star. Finishing his drink he got up and slipped out quickly while Hatcher was buying another beer. Devane's habit of studying faces, had paid off on more than one occasion. He had a feeling this deputy whose name he remembered was Hatcher, was trouble. He went to the telegraph office and asked the operator if there was a message for Carruthers.

'Surely, came this morning after you was asking,' the small man with a nervous tic told him and handed Devane a piece of paper. The message read: 'Goods believed despatched two days ago after your departure. Take care. JB'.

Smiling to himself, Devane walked off to the rooming-house where he had stayed last year. So, Mondell was on his way. He would probably stay well hidden somewhere. Had Hatcher anything to do with Mondell? Was he just after Buckland believing he would lead him to the $8,500? There was no way of knowing if he worked for the law or for himself. It seemed ominous that he had come to Yuma at this time. It meant he would have two of them to deal with. Thinking it through, Devane believed it might be a good idea to watch Hatcher. He could do nothing else until Buckland came out. The worst fear was that Louis Mondell was going to have Buckland arrested and then taken back to Baltimore. He doubted it was what he wanted. Perhaps he is going to get Hatcher to shoot Buckland while trying to escape. That would be more likely. The more he thought about it, the more he felt afraid. He got off the bed and went in search of Sheriff Baker. He found him in his office. 'You got a minute?' he asked and slid into a chair in front of the desk.

Baker looked up in surprise as he recognized who had asked the question. 'I reckon I have. Didn't expect to see you around here again,' he said warily.

Devane spoke quietly. 'A certain person is to be released on the 21st August from the prison. I am here to see that he is not impeded in any way in his departure from this town. I would be happy to, let's say, be fairly generous in rewarding yourself and the warden if it could be arranged for the release to be somewhat advanced. After all, the day starts after midnight.'

Baker gave a brief smile. 'So it's not

minerals this time you'll be looking for. Figured that wasn't your real line. You offering me a bribe?'

Devane felt uneasy. 'Someone sent word to a certain person about the release date. He's arrived somewhere, I'm sure. You remember the gun-fight last year?'

'Sure do! You reckon the dude is back? Never knew why he was in a place like this hick town. I guess you got an interest in this Jonas Buckland. Just who the hell is he? He's caused plenty of bother. He some big wig's son or something. Though he's been chummy with a Mexican who was more than just a peon. He croaked a couple of weeks ago. Pike told me; he sometimes has a beer with me when he comes into town.'

'I guess Buckland will be in bad shape then. Will he be able to ride?' Devane asked worriedly.

'Might be. He's been sick, I understand. Pike is mean, and the guards. There was one who wasn't bad. He helped them two, some.'

'Is there a chance you might see this Pike

146

and ask him if he would let Buckland out early, in the dark? Then I can get him away and lay up somewhere till he feels a bit better? I'm sure the warden would be happy to receive a token of Buckland's appreciation. He can't make a hell of a lot for the lousy job.'

'I reckon he wouldn't say no. I got a couple of kids needing new duds. One's ten, the other eight. Both boys. Get through a lot of britches they does.'

Grinning, Devane put a hand in his pocket and drew out $200 and slid it across to Baker. 'Give what you think to Pike. If he asks for more, let me know. Buy the kids some new duds as you wish; a present from their Uncle Clint. By the way, the deputy from Benson is also in town. Seems odd, don't you think?'

Baker looked at Devane. 'Yeah, that do seem odd! I better keep an eye on him. Thanks! You take care! I'll be in touch, you're at Walt's rooming-house, right?'

Still grinning, Devane went out, his hat pulled low and went off to his room and pulled out a bottle and sank on to his bed.

Baker, he thought, didn't miss much that went on in Yuma.

After he left the cafe, Hatcher took his horse to the livery stable and asked the ostler to give him some grain. He also asked if he could stay up top for the night and tossed him two dollars. He lay up in the loft till around seven o'clock then went to get some food. Mondell was camped along the Gila River. He would ride out and see him when he had something to tell him. After he had eaten he went to the saloon which was full of the usual sort of drifters and such that rode through Yuma. Their eyes were furtive and often bloodshot, and their language as unsavoury as it could get. There were four guards, Hatcher noticed, playing dominoes at a table. He took his beer over and sat next to them. Later, a man in new levis and smiling broadly, came over to sit with them.

'Jeez, Collins,' one of the guards said. 'You always was the lucky one. Hear you got a job already.'

The thin, hollow eyed man of medium height, though almost a bantam weight now, answered the guard. 'Yep, I start next week on the Prescott run. I'm sleeping at the stage-line livery, looking after the horses till I take up the shot-gun job.'

'Did Pike give you the ten dollars you're supposed to get when you leave? You was a prisoner, after all.'

'Yeah, he give it me. He let me have these duds. When I've saved a bit, I'm heading for San Francisco. Maybe get a job on a ship. I always wanted to go to China.' Collins laughed and sat down to talk.

It was not long before the guards got up and left. Collins sat over a beer. He had little left of the ten dollars having got through two bottles to celebrate his release, and he had to eat.

Hatcher leaned over to him. 'Can I buy you another?' he asked. 'Couldn't help overhearing about your new job. I guess it must have been hard guarding those renegades up on that hill?' he added.

Collins hesitated. 'Mister I'm skint, I

can't buy you none back,' he said.

'Hell, that don't matter! I just need a bit of company. I'm passing through.' Hatcher called to the barman. 'Bring a bottle.'

By the time Hatcher and Collins left the saloon, Collins was hardly able to walk. Hatcher got him to his bunk bed at the tack room at the stage-line livery. Collins had told Hatcher what he wanted to know. One thing that had come out though, was the fact Buckland was being released on Wednesday which was the 21st not the 22nd. Mondell would be interested in that. He went to get his horse telling the ostler he had to visit a farmer he knew and would probably be back.

Mondell, who was sitting with his back against his saddle heard Hatcher coming and got up pulling his Colt. One could not be too careful, he thought. Hatcher gave two short whistles before he rode in and Mondell gave two in answer.

'I got some news for you,' Hatcher said as he swung down. 'Buckland is coming out the 21st, not the 22nd. I got it from an ex-guard. He finished last week. Got

150

a job with the stage line. He told me, after I got him plenty drunk, that they let prisoners out after the warden gets up, usually after nine, or could be later. He has to sign the release and he don't do that till the morning.'

Hatcher looked surprised at how Mondell had coped. 'I see you ain't no greenhorn at making a camp,' he said and helped himself to some coffee.

'I spent three years at West Point, then I left because I couldn't stand the bullshit,' Mondell replied. He was glad he had brought Hatcher with him. 'Well we have two days instead of three, that is better. You can go back and keep your ears open. I will meet you around midnight on the 20th. I'll come in to the rear of the staging line barn. I'll do a bit of a recce around in the meantime.'

Devane had observed Hatcher from where he sat at the back of the saloon. It was pretty clear what he was after now. He slipped out behind Hatcher when he left holding Collins up. He saw him take him to the stage-line livery and then come out again and go to the main livery barn. A few minutes later he came out again. In a hurry, Devane got his horse saddled and got mounted. The moon was up and he could see a vague shape heading off towards the Gila River. After Hatcher had disappeared down a short defile he saw the brief flicker of a camp fire. He got off his horse and went on foot up the shallow wash which ran from the river, but was dry now for the summer. It was not light enough to see who the other man was, but he felt satisfied that it would be Mondell. He mounted when he got back to his horse and went back to town. In two days those two would surface. He must be ready with a plan.

On the morning of the second day, Devane found a note had been delivered for him by hand. He read it through while he had his breakfast. 'Meet me at the ferry around noon, Baker', the note read.

At midday Devane waited in some shade watching the ferry being hauled across. A little before one o'clock Baker came riding up the trail. He swung down by the ferryman's hut and came across to where Devane sat. He had his canteen with him and sat down on the tree bole which was rotted, next to Devane. 'I got delayed,' he said passing the canteen. Then he pulled out a stogey.

'Pike's agreed. He wanted a hundred. He's a mean devil. Says he'll be glad to be rid of Buckland. It'll be afore daylight. Didn't say exactly what time. I hope he keeps his word. Buckland is in bad shape I heard from one of the guards. Had dysentery. He'll be needing rest and just plain food for a long time.'

'Yes, I know. I once had the Montezuma's revenge when in Mexico. It is not very pleasant,' Devane said remembering how ill he had been.

'What is it with this Buckland? Who the hell is he? Why's there so much interest in him?'

'I think it's a vendetta. A more classy type of an Arkansas hillmen's feud, you could say.' Devane gave a brief smile.

'Well, I'll be damned!' Baker chuckled. 'I'll do my best to see there's no gunplay in my town. You get him across the river, that'd be best. Head for the first train stop. They're busy with the new line and soon it'll come over the river. I gotta go. You be careful on Wednesday morning.' Baker looked hard at Devane.

Devane shook Baker's hand. 'You too, Sheriff, you take care of your kids. See they grow up good,' he said. Baker, he figured, would be a good man to have at one's side if there was trouble.

TEN

Hawk Fernandez was lying on a rock ledge under an overhang in a dry wash. He was thinking about Buckland and hoping nothing would go wrong with his release. He hoped he would be able to see him and thank him for getting him out. He could still hardly believe that he was a free man. After lying in that coffin, wondering if Pike was playing some dreadful joke on him, he had woken up sweating the first few nights, and once had screamed till the Mexican peon he had taken shelter with in his adobe house had come and reassured him that he was no longer a prisoner. When he had walked away and gone down river and found Pepe Lopez, he had been on the verge of collapse. Pepe had taken him in and looked after him. He had fed him on goats' milk, beans and chicken stew. He had refused to take the two dollars and asked no questions.

Two weeks of rest and a couple of meals a day had done wonders for him. He was still weak though and exertion tired him easily. After he had seen Jonas, then what? He had only the two dollars. His clothing was threadbare. It would be difficult to get work. If he could get to Monterey in California and locate a friend of his late father, he might be able to help. It was a long way to go and if he didn't eat regularly he would soon be ill again.

Jonas had been vague about his past. Would he have someone to meet him when he came out? The uncle surely would come to help him, bring money. Pike might not give him the ten dollars he should get. Without stage or train fare, where could one go in this dried up terrain? Tonight, Hawk thought, he would pick a spot and lay in hiding till Jonas came out and watch to see if someone did contact him. He must be careful though because if one of the guards saw him it would go hard for him. It would also be difficult for Pike. He would lie and say he had escaped at the cemetery...that's what he would do. Then they would put him back in that cell and leave him to rot. Hawk shivered.

A voice spoke from above the ledge. He jumped and lay quite still.

'Hey, *amigo!* What're you doing under there?'

Should he try to run for it? Play it cool, it didn't sound like one of the guards. A horse came off the rim into the wash. 'You been taking a siesta under there? I hope you checked for scorpions and snakes first,' Paul Devane said in a friendly vein. He got down off the horse, pulled out a couple of small cigars and offered one. 'You care for a smoke?'

'*Si señor,*' Fernandez grovelled a little.

Devane sat down on the ledge and offered a light watching the peon's uneasy glances up and down the wash. He looked as if he were about to bolt.

Fernandez was wondering who the man was. Earlier he had seen the very same horse heading southwards. Just who was he? What was this man after? He wore a side gun, heavy strong laced up boots and strong cotton, hunting type clothes.

'Is there a settlement down river?' Devane asked, switching into Spanish.

Surprised, Hawk said he thought not, until one came to the border.

Devane had caught sight of the sores on Fernandez' legs, and now saw he was emaciated, his eyes sunken. In fact, he looked very much like one of the prisoners he had observed in the rock pit. Surely he couldn't be an escapee. 'You from around these parts?' he enquired.

'No. I was visiting a friend. I go over

the river I wait for him. Tomorrow he will come.'

'I see!' said Devane, giving the Mexican a strange look. Something clicked in his memory. The man was tall he could see. He sure as hell looked like the one who had been next to Buckland breaking rocks. 'Nasty sores you have. Were you in that hell hole breaking rocks?' He looked directly at Fernandez.

Fernandez' eyes slitted, his face went hard. He knew this man would not be deceived if he denied it. 'I was in there. Now I am out.'

'Did you by any chance know a man called Jonas Buckland?' Again Devane looked directly at him.

Hawk was cautious in his reply. 'I might have. Is he a friend of yours?'

'Not a friend. I have never met him. He comes out tomorrow. Is he the friend you wait for?'

'Why do you want to know this? I think I must leave now, *señor*,' Hawk said coolly.

'Hey, don't go off in a huff. If you are the Mexican friend of Jonas, then you can

158

help me. I wish to get him away safe. There are two men who are already here waiting who wish to do him harm.'

Hawk gave a brief smile but he was still cautious. 'It is possible, *señor*, that you may be one of those men. How can I be sure you are not?'

'I expect Jonas gave you some of his little extras that his uncle brought for him. Listen, I have money for him and a horse which I have left further along this wash. Come on, let's go before someone else finds him. I will tell you what I want you to do. I also have food. You look as if you can do with some. I know the hell you have gone through in that rotten place. Jonas will be in poor shape. I hear that he has been ill.'

Devane took the reins of the horse and walked along the wash and Fernandez followed him. Jonas was expecting someone to meet him, he was sure of that. This man, he felt sure, was genuine. He would watch him though. The thought of food had him hastening his steps.

Devane got a low fire going and handed

Hawk a tin of beans. 'I'm sorry it's beans, but I have bread and cheese too. Have you any money?'

'Two dollars, and this suit which belonged to a dead man. I am grateful for the food, *señor.*'

'My name is Paul. You need not know anything more about me. What is yours, if I may ask?'

'Felipé, but everyone calls me Hawk. It was once said I had the eyes of the hawk, so it has stuck.' Fernandez laughed.

'Have you and Jonas worked out a plan for when you got out?' Devane asked casually.

'No! It was not sure that I would get away safely.' Hawk replied then coloured up.

'You mean you weren't let out?' Devane gasped.

'I came out in a coffin. I was supposed to be dead. Now I *am* officially dead. I do not exist!'

'Good God! How did you manage it?'

'I am not sure. I think Jonas fixed it. I think he must have paid the warden something, or is going to. I cannot see how he would have allowed it unless he got plenty of dinero.'

Devane chuckled. 'I think I am going to like your friend Jonas. We must see he gets safely away. And you too. We will work out a plan together. We will get some sleep till it gets dark. I must also get a horse for you. I will take you to the ferryman's hut and you will wait in a brake where you can watch the trail.'

At the time Paul Devane and Hawk Fernandez were devising their plan of action, and getting acquainted, Louis Mondell and Jed Hatcher were a few miles north by the Gila River, also making plans.

Meantime, the subject of their plans of action was in a state of nervous and physical collapse. To be free from this pest hole was enough excitement, but the added worry as to whether Mondell was out there waiting for him was difficult to cope with.

Buckland had decided he would head

straight for town and the sheriff's office. Mondell could hardly come in there unless he told the sheriff that there was a warrant out for him. He would not get his chance to kill him that way. If no one turned up to help him, he would have only ten dollars and what he stood up in. Pike might decide not to give him the statutory ten dollars. He would want the money for letting Hawk out, so he probably would give it to him. For the past two days he had been let off rock breaking and given a little more food, not that it was any better. He had slept little since Collins had left. He was in pretty bad shape. Tonight would be his last night in prison. He said a silent prayer as the men returned from the rock pit.

Before they were locked in for the night, a guard came for Buckland and took him over to the farrier who took off the leg irons, and was none too gentle.

'Put these clothes on,' the guard, Wilkins, told him. Then he took him back to his bunk and locked him in, giving no explanation of any kind.

Devane and Fernandez were waiting at the ferry. It was the last crossing until seven in the morning.

'Now you watch out for yourself when you get across. Find a good place to hide where you can see the trail. If all goes to plan we should be coming across on the first ferry. If we haven't come, let's say by nightfall, you keep the horse and ride on. It will be better if you get away from here as far as you can. Here is fifty dollars. Take care, *amigo*,' Devane told Hawk.

Hawk shook hands with Devane and thanked him with some emotion. Perhaps the Lord had sent this man to help him. 'I hope you will come, *señor*. I would like to know that Jonas is safe.' He stepped on to the ferry and Jess Haskell roped him across. He had been finished for the day and about to go to bed when Devane came and asked him to take the Mexican over. A twenty dollar gold piece had been the persuader.

Devane waited until Haskell came back again. It was quite chilly now. He pulled a bottle from a saddle bag and invited

Haskell to join him in a drink. After he had tied up the ferry, they went into the shack and sat by the stove where Haskell took his whiskey in a tin mug and poured coffee to mix with it.

'If I were to come about six in the morning with a friend, would you be willing to take us over early?' he asked the ferryman.

'Might!' Haskell said. 'But if you're toting jail birds as looks like they was on the run, then maybe I ain't too keen.'

'I assure you they are not escaped prisoners. Some do come out, you know. Not everyone in there is guilty of a crime. Sometimes the law makes mistakes. I will pay you another gold piece, if I do get here early, that was all I was asking,' Devane said wearily.

'If you come early, then I'll take you across. You'll maybe have to wake me first,' Haskell replied.

Buckland was lying on his back on his bunk and fretting. Two men were snoring loudly. He felt cold and he had no idea

what time it was in the pitch black cell.
His head throbbed and he felt sick with
hunger. Suddenly a key turned in the
lock. The iron barred gate clanked open.
Someone came with a lamp and looked at
one or two bunks then a face peered over
him. It was Wilkins who shook him. 'Get
up Buckland. You got your clothes on? If
not, then get dressed and hurry.'

A voice from the rear shouted, 'What
the hell is going on?'

Wilkins barked back. 'Shut up and mind
your own business. Go back to sleep.'

Scrambling quickly out behind Wilkins
after putting on the tight fitting boots
he had been given with the ill-fitting
suit, Buckland caught up with the guard.
Without the leg irons he felt strange and
unbalanced. He had been used to walking
with short steps. 'Wilkins! Am I going out?
What about my own things I had when I
came in?'

'I don't have nothing for you. Pike gave
me your signed release paper. Here, take it.
Don't lose it. He told me you was to go to
the sheriff's office and wait there. I guess

somebody will be meeting you.' Wilkins growled and led him across the yard to the stockade gate where he shouted to a guard in a shack.

The guard, after checking the note from Pike, opened the gate a fraction. Wilkins gave Buckland a hard shove and he went plummeting downwards till he sprawled on his face some yards down the track. Slowly he pulled himself up and got to his feet. For a few minutes he just stood there getting accustomed to the less dark atmosphere. He suddenly had a strong desire to yell out loud but he quickly rejected the idea. Why had he been let out in the middle of the night? Go to the sheriff's office, Wilkins had said. He started to walk and felt the cold. Pike had not given him his ten dollars nor his silver watch back. There was nothing he could do about it. All he had was five dollars he had secreted away in his pallet. If there was no one to meet him he would not get far on five dollars. He began to feel afraid as he walked unsteadily down the hill. What if Mondell was out there somewhere waiting? Pike had trusted him about the money so he would not want him killed.

The dark shapes of the town ahead of him became clearer as he got closer. He wondered where Hawk was. Is he safe in Mexico? He had said he would look for me. He stumbled over a stone and almost went down again. A cock crowed from somewhere and a dog barked. It must soon be daylight he thought. People would be emerging from their homes. What would they think if they saw him looking so dishevelled, smelling so high? He had not seen anything of the town. He passed a hotel and saw a sign that said Bath House. Oh if only it were open now! A barber's shop too. If there was no one to meet him he would have to send a message to Kingsley then wait hidden somewhere till the money was telegraphed through to the bank. What if he could get to Benson and see Doc Hughes? He had $1,000 of his money. It would not be sensible to go there. Still, he could telegraph him perhaps.

The sheriff's office was there on his left. He went over to it but the door was locked. Of course it would be at this time of night. Kingsley must know of his release date, he would have made sure Pike let him know, or perhaps the sheriff.

A sound of hoofbeats made him move along the boardwalk away from the office. He went to the corner and stood in a doorway recess. A shape appeared in the street. A horse and rider came on up the centre and passed right on by him. Should he have called out? Was the rider looking for him? The horse disappeared along the trail towards the prison. Still Buckland stayed in the deep shadow. There were a few halos of light from the lamps. There was another sound, this time it was one of the boards squeaking as a figure walked to the sheriff's office and stopped. Someone coughed softly. A voice called out 'Johnny' very soft but clear. Only his sisters had ever called him that. Of course Mondell would know that. What if it were him? Should he reveal himself?

Devane stalked like a cat as he came towards the corner from where he had detected a small sound. He held his hunting knife in his right hand. He halted a few feet from the doorway where he was sure there was someone waiting. 'Marcus Kingsley sent me,' he whispered. 'Buckland, come out if it is you.'

Buckland took a couple of steps forward. In his hand was a stone he had picked up when he'd stumbled.

'Are you the one who was here last year?' he whispered back.

'Yes!' Devane stepped up to Buckland. 'Thank God you are out early! Come on, I have horses round the back.' He led the way down the cross street and came to the rear of a store where two horses stood, heads drooping. 'Do you think you are able to ride?'

'I'm not sure. I cannot walk very well. But I will have to, won't I?'

'We'll give it a try, we are heading for the ferry and across the river.' Devane took hold of Buckland's arm and handed him up into the saddle of his own horse, which in the darkness he did not recognize. Devane got mounted and led the way down the back street heading out on the trail to the ferry.

By the time they reached the ferryman's shack, Buckland was ready to fall off. He clutched at the pommel. 'I don't think I can ride far,' he said apologetically. 'I have dysentery. My bowels are burning.'

'Listen, Buckland. It is imperative we get over the river and cover some miles then we can probably hide some place till you get some rest and some decent food into you. There are two men in Yuma who are waiting for you to come out. That is why you were let out early. The sheriff made a deal with Pike.'

Buckland swayed and Devane took hold of him and got him down out of the saddle and helped him over to a bench in front of the shack. 'Rest here. I'm going to wake the ferryman. He will take us across early. It is just gone 5.30 a.m. The first ferry goes at seven. We will have almost two hours start at least. When they find

170

out you are already out they will most likely decide you have gone west. I said Kingsley sent me, in fact, it was your father.' Devane spoke quietly. Then he opened the door and went inside and shook Haskell who was sleeping soundly on his bunk. Then he put the coffee pot on the stove and thrust some logs in through the door at the front and got the fire going.

Haskell got up slowly, grumbling. Devane put the gold coin into his hands. 'If you could hurry my friend, I'd be grateful.'

Buckland had managed to get some rather dry bread into his stomach and a coffee laced with whiskey. He coughed as it went down. It revived him some. Then they were on to the ferry and hauling on the rope and ten minutes later were on the other side.

'If an eastern gent and a hick come asking about us, you tell them you never saw us. They aren't very nice people, so take care, and thanks, Haskell,' Devane told the ferryman who nodded, yawned and set off back across the river.

ELEVEN

As Hatcher rode up the street and headed for the spot he had picked out to await the release of Buckland, Mondell rode in behind the livery stable of the stage line. He was no longer concerned that Sheriff Baker might happen to spot him. It was hardly likely he would be around so early. There was only one way Buckland would be taking if he were walking. If there was someone waiting with a horse Hatcher would surely see whoever it was. Buckland would not be heading out into the real desert. Nor was he likely to take the stage or train. To get away from Yuma and disappear as quickly as possible he would be riding. Someone had collected his horse, so that person must be waiting. Hatcher had been unable to say if any of the strangers in town might be the one. Buckland would need money wherever he

172

went. Perhaps Baker was holding some for him. Why had he given him the wrong date for Buckland's release? It was lucky Hatcher had discovered the error.

The town was beginning to stir. It was just gone six and it was still quite cold. There was a sound of buckets rattling, horses whinnying from within the barn. An aroma of coffee drifted out and hit Mondell's nostrils as he leaned against an old stage coach, its wheels broken, a door sagging. He could see the trail leading down from the prison. How long would he have to wait now for Buckland to appear? Impatiently, Mondell took out a cheroot, struck a match on the broken wheel and lit it.

Hawk Fernandez saw the ferry bring Devane and his old friend Buckland across the river, as he hid in amongst some reeds. His heart was pounding as he left his hide out and went back to untie his horse and then hauled himself up into the saddle of the rather ageing animal that Devane had managed to purchase in something of a hurry after they had made their plans. A buggy with two men seated on the spring seat came down the trail followed by three riders who looked like rangemen. Hawk waited before he came out from the cluster of bushes.

Devane saw Hawk come on to the trail and relaxed a little as he recognized him. He turned to Buckland who was holding onto the horn and looking as if he might collapse at any moment. 'We have company,' he called to him.

Startled, Buckland raised his head to gaze along the trail. His bloodshot eyes took in the Mexican peon on the sway-backed horse. There was something familiar about him. As he got closer his features slid into a wide grin. 'It's Hawk! *Amigo! Cómo está usted?*' he called out hoarsely.

'*Bien! Gracias!*' Hawk replied, his face gone grave as he saw the condition Buckland was in.

'That's a hell of a horse you have there.' Buckland tried to hide the emotion he felt on seeing his friend again; to know he was all right. Now he knew he could go on. He had to.

'It's the best I could get at short notice. I didn't know I was going to run into your *amigo*. He's been a great help watching the river while I waited for you to come out. Now we must get on. Your old friend Mondell is in town, and Deputy Hatcher. They'll be waiting somewhere watching the prison. It probably won't take them long to discover you were let out early. We have the sheriff to thank for that,' said Devane.

Buckland looked surprised then worried. 'Hatcher, so he's here as well. That doesn't surprise me. I expect he thinks you have brought the money from the bank robbery, since you collected my horse.'

'Hatcher does not know who collected the horse. He will only be guessing. I should think Mondell has hired him. He would not wish to show his face in Yuma.'

They had walked almost half a mile when Devane asked Buckland if he could manage a steady lope. 'If we can put some distance behind us and then get in some place where you can rest. You will need to eat, but only a little at a time until you can hold it down,' Devane told Buckland.

Buckland had not asked questions. He simply put what little strength he had into keeping himself in the saddle. The knowledge that Hatcher and Mondell might appear on the skyline behind them at any time was enough to put the fear of God into him. He put all his faith in this man who had come to help him. Hawk, he could see, was still in a weakened condition. The idea of Hatcher coming upon them worried him more than being confronted by Louis Mondell. Not that he believed Mondell wouldn't carry out his threat to kill him, but he thought Hatcher would be more trigger happy. There was no love lost between Hatcher and him.

When Hatcher came loping down the trail and pulled in behind the livery, Mondell could see he was fuming as he slid to a halt. 'That stinking warden went and let Buckland out early. He's gone. A guard on the stockade told me.' Hatcher swung down.

'What time did he come out?' Mondell asked, his mind making some swift calculations.

'About five o'clock, and apparently he was walking down the trail like a drunken man. He's in bad shape!'

'Come on!' Mondell grabbed his horse's reins and went walking off. 'We'll check the hotels and rooming-houses. Then you check the Mexican adobes. He can't have taken a stage or train. Neither is due out yet. I expect he's gone by horse, perhaps northwards. After we've searched we'll have some breakfast. I'm damned hungry.'

Sheriff Baker was standing in his office doorway when he saw Mondell slip into the hotel. Of all the gall. It certainly looked as if they had missed Buckland's early release. This time the easterner had brought a gunhand with him it seemed. Calling to his deputy, Howard Sprague, that he would be gone for a while, Baker untied his horse and stepped into the saddle and loped off westwards. He was sure Buckland and his contact would not go south for Mexico. He'd be more likely to go west to the man who'd visited him in prison. An uncle, so Pike had said. He loped on down the trail and came up to the ferryman's shack and dismounted as Jess Haskell hailed him. 'You want coffee, George?'

'Yep! I reckon that would be nice!' Baker tied his horse to a post and went inside with Haskell.

'You interested in anything particular? Don't often see you out this early.' Haskell gave Baker a guarded look.

'You taken any strangers over first thing? A fella in one of them hunting-type jackets, and one as might look rather worse for wear?' Baker returned Haskell's casual question with one of his own.

'Was a couple; they came early. I was still in bed. The first one you mentioned paid me extra. I reckon the other one, well he was real sick. Like he just came out of that hell hole. You don't think he could've escaped? Ain't never seen one yet as got

178

away. Them as run for it, they goes south mostly, and dies in that desert.' Haskell told Baker what he wanted to know.

'Nope. I'm not going after them. Nobody's escaped. They're out of my territory now. There's probably another couple might come soon. I'll stick around a bit Jess. If they come asking questions you tell 'em you haven't seen those two you took across.'

Haskell took a bottle of whiskey out from a cupboard. 'Bit chilly this morning. You fancy a touch?' he asked Baker. 'Might be a good idea if you was to stick around,' he added uneasily.

Hatcher and Mondell spent an hour searching and asking questions in the town. The deputy told Hatcher he hadn't been up till around eight. He reckoned someone might have given the released prisoner a lift in a wagon some place.

Mondell was fuming as they ate a quick breakfast at the cafe. As he watched Hatcher devour bacon, eggs and a stack of hot cakes, he felt ready to leave him behind. He would know the terrain though, probably know where to find water.

'They'll have gone over the river, I reckon,' Hatcher said, his mouth full of hot cake.

'I've been thinking that also. Look, I'll need you a while longer. We can ride faster than they'll be able to move. Buckland will be in a weak state. My guess is they'll hole up for perhaps two or three days once they are clear and out into that vast territory. We should be able to find them. What do you think?' Mondell asked, and called for the bill.

'They'll build a fire at night. There ain't much till they get to El Centro. They can get the train there. That's what the station fella told me.' Hatcher got up and followed Mondell outside. 'I'll be wanting more dough if it takes a lot longer. We'll find them two. They don't know this country like I do. Them easterners ain't used to the heat like we gets in Arizona and lower California. There's miles of nothing out there. They could be dead in two days if they don't find the water holes.'

'All right, Hatcher! You find them and I'll pay you extra. I don't have a lot of time to waste,' Mondell snapped and got on to his horse.

Baker was sitting inside the shack when Mondell and Hatcher showed up around ten o'clock. He stayed inside when he saw Hatcher gesticulating in what he could only describe as aggressive fashion. He checked his side-gun. Jess had a shortish fuse, he might just start something. A few minutes later Haskell and the two men went on to the ferry when a stage wagon arrived and four passengers also got aboard. Baker sighed and went out and mounted his horse. Well, they were at least four hours behind Buckland and his friend who looked as if he might be quite capable of handling himself in a tight spot. He loped on back to town in a relieved frame of mind.

Paul Devane looked back worriedly. He had caught up with Buckland and the Mexican. Both were hardly fit for some really good hard riding. Buckland was hung over the horn. He had had to stop once or twice and disappear behind a bush. Hawk looked at Devane. 'I think we must get off the trail and rest. Jonas is in bad shape,' he said.

'Yes, it is getting hot now too. He probably hasn't slept for days, and he needs food. Something bland. Rice if we can get it.' Devane took out his field glasses and studied the terrain. 'There's a dry creek bed running south over there, we'll head for that and lay up till it gets cooler. You two can get some sleep. According to a rough map the ostler made for me, there's a small settlement a few miles on. I'd like to get as far as that and buy some more provisions and see if there is another route to El Centro. If we see no sign of Mondell following we can board the train there and be into Los Angeles in a day or two.'

Hawk nodded. 'I will cover the tracks where we leave the trail,' he said and got down. Devane threw him his knife to cut a small bush to drag over their hoof marks, though they were only visible here and there on the hard ground.

They found a good place about two miles away from the trail where the creek bed was deep enough for them not to be seen from a distance. They ate cold beans and cheese. Devane handed his whiskey bottle to Buckland. 'It will help drive out the bug. Later I'll get brandy. A few hours sleep will help you, both of you. I'll keep an eye out.'

'What if they are on our trail, they'll ride past us won't they?' Buckland asked warily.

'That is possible. That is why I want to go into the settlement later, when it gets dark. Any strangers will be sure to draw attention. Someone always notices them. What else have they to amuse themselves with?' Devane smiled. 'Don't worry. If they don't see us, they will press on for El Centro and most likely wait there. Or, they may think we didn't come this way and go back.'

Hawk spoke up. 'If they offer the ferryman plenty of dinero, I think he will tell them we crossed. Why does this man wish to kill you?' He turned and looked at Buckland.

'He hates me, it is an old score. It is the deputy who worries me most now. He believes I really took that money. Why else would he be here?'

'As Hawk has just said,' Devane interjected, 'most folks have their price. Hatcher will have been bought. Mondell is shrewd enough to know he has little experience of this western land. He will also have reckoned that someone would be coming to help you. Now, both of you get some sleep.' Devane took charge. He got his rifle from its boot and walked northwards up the creek bed.

Devane found himself a spot on the rim of the creek next to a prickly pear, in its shade. He sat for some time using the glasses. Nothing much stirred. The heat shimmered across the land. After about an hour he moved down into the wash and placed himself with his back to a protruding rock and pulled his hat over his face and dozed. A small antelope woke him later, and he put his hand quickly to the rifle. The animal leapt up the other side and was gone. The sun had moved round and he strode on back down the wash. Both men were sound asleep. Again he used the glasses and scoured the terrain and saw nothing.

TWELVE

Sweat dripped off the end of Mondell's nose. He turned to Hatcher as they slowed down the pace they had been riding at for over an hour. They had found a watering hole and stopped for a breather, and Hatcher had made enquiries of the man and woman who were encamped there.

'There be three of them,' the man told him.

'Three! Are you sure they were like I described? One of them must have looked real sickly.' Hatcher eyed the man keenly.

'Oh yes!' the woman spoke up. 'One was in a real bad way. He looked so thin

185

and his clothes worn and didn't fit him. The Mexican looked thin too. He and the better dressed one; they were talking in Spanish,' she said positively. 'The clean one had a suit like them army men wear in Mexico...well it could have been a hunting jacket like I seen some of them men wears as comes from Europe.'

Mondell had nodded. 'We're obliged to you ma'am.' They had watered the horses, filled their canteens and moved on quickly.

'I believe now that the thin Mexican must be the one I saw in the rock pit, and the other man someone who was sent with money etc. I have an idea who he is. Last year there was a man called Carruthers who said he was prospecting,' Mondell said to Hatcher.

'An' I bet he was the one who took Buckland's horse. You reckon they'll be heading over the border and maybe down to the gulf and get on a boat? They could go any where they liked from the Pacific,' Hatcher opined. 'I reckon we best let the horses have some rest. It's hot now, and my guess is they'll be doing the same.'

Mondell agreed. After some coffee, bread and cheese, he stretched out and closed his eyes. Perhaps there was something in what Hatcher had said. But on the other hand, why would Buckland have come back to America? No, he was probably heading for Los Angeles and possibly to San Francisco. He thought of the rivalry between his own family and the Benedicts. Both in business and in society, it had always been so. The Benedicts were richer, they had a shipping line and offices on both east and west coasts. Damn it! Somewhere out there was Buckland regaining his strength. If he didn't find him now he would be gone for good. Then he would have failed. The sky had gone darkish, and clouds were heading towards them. Come what may he would go on to Los Angeles and San Francisco and back home. Hatcher gave him a prod.

'There's a storm coming, we'd better move on.' he advised.

By late afternoon the storm swept over.

Devane and his charges had moved under an overhang in a hollow. After it had passed, creeks and gulleys were swollen to overflowing and water spreading out was soaked down into the earth and drooping foliage lifted up their branches once again.

Buckland had slept almost four hours before they had set off again heading for the small settlement which was now only about a mile away. Devane, who had been searching the terrain with his fieldglasses came back to them. 'We may as well stay here. I can see the few adobes and a shack or two. I will go in later and stock up with what I can buy there.'

Hawk agreed. 'It is best. Jonas needs more rest. It is possible this Mondell and his partner will be ahead of us now, or soon will be. If they are following. They will also make enquiries at the village. Perhaps it would be better if you wore my clothes when you go in, and speak Spanish.'

Devane grinned. 'Good idea! When the sun has gone down I will go. There is a spare shirt and pants in my duffel bag, and clothes for Jonas. You two keep warm. I will leave the rifle and wear my side-gun. You will find another revolver in the bag. Give it to Jonas, just in case.'

It was almost dark as Devane rode out and went into the village. He located a small store and pulled up in front of it, after seeing there were no other horses tethered anywhere. Devane still had on his own pants, but the top he had borrowed from Fernandez smelled none too sweet. Underneath it he wore a money belt. If anyone should decide to dry-gulch him, they would be surprised at what it contained. He wondered if it looked odd his wearing a sidearm, and that he rode a good horse. They might believe him to be a bandit from across the border. He fervently hoped he would not run into Mondell.

There wasn't a lot of choice in the store. He took some flat bread, goat cheese and dried fruit. Some tins of the inevitable beans. Next he went to the cantina. The place stank of chilli and body sweat. He sat at a table and ordered a meal. It consisted of chunks of meat and chilli beans and bread. Spurning the coffee he ordered tequila and shuddered as it burnt his gullet. From the man behind the rough bar he bought a bottle of Mexican brandy, and he got the woman who had brought his food to wrap up half a dozen tortillas and some meat which he figured he could cook tomorrow. He also asked an old man who sat outside on a bench, if he had seen two men pass through, or if they had stopped off, one riding a roan horse. The man told him he had seen only three vaqueros from a ranchero to the south. Devane gave him two bits and got mounted.

Stars were beginning to show as he rode back the way he had come, but quite a distance before he came to the camp he began to circle. He thought he had heard a bit jangle. A soft wind was coming from the south as he headed back to the trail. He turned east and rode at a quick walk. He was quite sure he had heard a horse blow down its nostrils. He went into a lope covering almost two miles before he eased up. He had gone past the large Joshua tree he used as a landmark before they had left the trail earlier. Very quickly he got down and led the horse off the trail some yards, then he got the horse to lie down and he lay holding its head down and covering its muzzle. Some minutes later a horse went loping on down the trail. Devane gave the rider about five minutes then he got up and led the horse westwards again going through scrub bush and up and down small hollows till he hit the creek where they had rested. It had almost dried up again. When he climbed out on to the rim he mounted and rode on for almost a mile. The moon was up and he could see the village silhouetted against the velvet sky. Before he went down into the hollow he gave two soft long whistles. He heard the reply from Hawk and got down leading the horse in behind the chaparral bush where the other two horses were tethered.

Hawk had been busy collecting bits of bush and wood for a fire. 'I did not think

I should light it till you came,' he told Devane.

'Better you didn't. I think I was followed. I think I lost whoever it was. He's gone down the east trail. If he was after me he'll not go too far when he doesn't catch up. I have some tortillas, cheese and bread. Also a bottle of brandy and more smokes,' Devane grinned.

Buckland was up on his feet and also grinning. 'I found a pool further down and gave myself a good wash before I put the new clothes on. By God, it feels good! Just getting some sleep has helped.'

'Eat the bread and cheese, and then take a good measure of brandy. Once we get your stomach right you will improve,' Devane advised. 'Tomorrow you will have meat and beans. Oh, I got a lemon to have with the tequila, and some salt.'

Hawk grinned. 'You have been in Mexico, my friend.'

'Yes, I've been there. I nearly got caught by the Federales. Now I will get some sleep. I have eaten. Hawk, you take first watch. Here is my watch. Wake me in three hours, sooner if necessary. Do not smoke or light the fire, and keep the horses quiet.'

Hawk nodded, but Buckland looked anxious. He did as Devane had bade him and ate bread and cheese. It was several hours now since he had last had to run. It was slowly beginning to dawn on him that he was a free man. If only he could get Mondell off his back he could really begin to enjoy himself in this wilderness, which he found fascinating and awesome.

Hatcher ran his horse for almost a mile then pulled him in. He had lost the Mex. Must have gone off some place, he muttered to himself. That meant he had probably gone to where the others were camped. It surely looked like they were heading for El Centro. Then where the hell else was there, if they weren't going over the border? Wasn't much over there neither. He turned his horse round and loped on back at a steady pace. It was lucky the storm had come. Without water in the heat that had hit this area, this summer, one could be dead in two days. As he rode, his eyes searched for sign of a campfire. If it was Buckland and the Mex, they would not light a fire, he thought. Well, it should be easy enough to find them tomorrow.

Hatcher went back to where Mondell was waiting, up a small draw north of the village.

He greeted him apprehensively. 'Did you have any luck?'

'Yep. A Mex was in the village. An old man told me. I just missed him, but I picked him up going down the trail. I think he must have heard me because he disappeared all of a sudden. I reckon they must be camped down a draw somewhere. We'll find 'em in the morning.'

'I hope you are right,' Mondell sat down again. He let Hatcher fix a meal of sidebacon and beans, and fresh fruit. After they had had coffee and a few shots of whiskey, they rolled up and went to sleep.

THIRTEEN

Hawk did not wake Devane till well after midnight. He had slept little of late and it was beginning to have its toll on him. As for himself, he was feeling more like a real human being again. To be able to think positively and make a decision was pure joy. He was far from fit but being involved with Devane and looking after his old friend, kept him from dwelling on the bitterness he might have let fester within him over losing eighteen months of his young life in that awful place. He shook Devane who woke up with a start and sat up quickly.

'Everything all right?' he asked as he stretched and got up.

'It is almost one o'clock. I let you sleep, you needed it.' Hawk told him. 'Shall I light a fire?'

'It is cold. I expect a hot drink would

195

do us no harm. We must be careful though. Sounds travel at night. Keep it low.' Devane walked off some yards.

Buckland also woke. 'Is it morning?' he asked.

'No, but it is another day,' Hawk replied. 'I am making coffee. We must not make too much noise in case our friends are out there some place.'

Devane came back and took the mug of coffee from Hawk. He laced it with a shot of brandy. A horse nickered and he stood very still listening. All three then became restless and Hawk went along to talk to them and calm them. When he came back Devane had doused the fire. 'It could be a bobcat,' Hawk said.

Devane said he would do a recce and told them to start packing up the gear. He went off with his rifle and disappeared walking without a sound. He was gone for some time. Facing west he stood next to a cholla and listened. There were rustling noises in the ground foliage, and a fluttering of wings. He had a strong feeling that someone was out there. Perhaps the

rider who had followed him. Hatcher and
Mondell would have pressed on once they
had crossed the river. They would almost
certainly have been to the village not too
long after he had been. Might even have
seen him. That seemed quite possible.

When he got back to the camp, Hawk
and Buckland were standing with the
horses waiting for his orders.

'I think we shall move on. We will lead
the horses south for a mile. I hope you feel
like a bit of walking. We are less likely to
be seen. Then we will swing west and get
on to the trail and ride as fast as you
two can.'

Buckland spoke then. 'I think Hawk
hasn't had any sleep. I feel much better.
It is up to him.'

'I slept through the day. I could not
sleep now. Paul is right, we ought to
press on, if we are to lose those two.'
Hawk urged them.

After they had saddled the horses and
tied on the gear, Devane led off down
the small fold. Soon they were moving on
parched rough grass which was dotted with

small bush, rocks and cactus. Buckland was stumbling so Devane called a halt.

'You all right?' he asked concernedly.

'It's these boots, they're too small.'

'We will ride now. As soon as we see a store or trading post, both of you can buy some decent footwear. I have money your father gave me,' Devane said to Jonas. 'Also eight hundred dollars Doc Hughes gave me. He took a hundred for the horse's keep, so I gave him a hundred more for being so honest.'

Buckland gave a wan smile. 'That was a good idea. Doc is a good man. He was very kind to me. I'm sorry you have become involved in all this. I don't want you to get hurt on my account. Perhaps at El Centro you could leave us. We'll manage all right.'

'It is my job and what I am being paid for. Any way, I have already decided to stay out west. I shall be heading for San Francisco. I think it is best you go there too. If we should get separated, stick with Hawk, he is a good hombre,' Devane explained.

'I know. He is my friend and he has no one. We shall stay together. We'll find something to do.'

Hawk, who had taken a short walk, came back. 'I have a feeling...I think I heard something,' he said.

'Let's get mounted.' Devane got up into his saddle. 'Just stay behind me in line. We are south of the village. Soon we should hit the trail then we can move on more quickly.'

Mondell and Hatcher got up well before dawn and after a quick coffee they struck camp and moved off. By the time it was light enough to see the trail and study it, Hatcher soon found evidence that three horses had recently moved along it. There were fresh droppings where they appeared to have stood for a while. They pressed on eagerly anticipating a sighting of the riders within the next hour or two. Mondell pulled himself out of the irritable mood he had been in after scratching himself on a prickly bush. He wanted the whole thing over so he could get back to a more civilized lifestyle. He utterly detested this wilderness and having to put up with Hatcher.

Devane had been forced to slow down. Hawk's mount couldn't maintain the pace of the other two. Buckland was hanging on to his horn in grim determination.

Pulling his fieldglasses, Devane surveyed the back trail, and then swung them round till he came to the trail ahead. 'There seems to be some boulders up yonder. We will stop there and build a fire. We will wait...set up an ambush. I do not think those two are ahead of us, I've seen no sign.'

Hawk, looking tired, said it was a good idea. 'Jonas is not well. He needs to rest again.'

When they came to the boulders where the trail ran through them, they found a grassy spot on the south side with some smaller rocks, and which looked as if it might have been a water hole at some time.

Devane got busy with his plan. Using the old clothes that the others had worn he stuffed them with brush then placed them against the rocks where Hawk had piled some brush and roots. 'We might as well have some coffee while we wait,' Devane told them. He also told Buckland to take the horses to the north side and hide them behind the twenty foot boulders where they wouldn't be seen from the trail.

Buckland came back after tethering the horses. 'I hope there won't be any gun-play. I don't think I could shoot at anyone. I'm sorry I'm not much help.'

'Both of you have done extremely well in the circumstances after what you have been through. You ought to be under a doctor's care now. I am sure this is the best way. I will try to get their horses then we take them and ride on. We'll hit the railroad soon and then be gone. They won't catch up!' He grinned and climbed up to a ledge out of the sun's glare. He searched the trail with the fieldglasses, but there was no one coming. He got down and took the mug of coffee Hawk passed to him and the tortilla stuffed with cold beans. What he could do to a plate full of steak and potatoes, he thought wistfully.

At the top of a long gradual rise, Mondell pulled up and got out the fieldglasses. They had ridden fairly hard after Hatcher had seen the droppings on the track. 'There's a ridge, a sort of rock formation up ahead. I think I see smoke.' He passed the glasses to Hatcher.

'Yep, that's a campfire. Could be cowpunchers or Mex peons with their sheep. Then again, it could be our friends cooking breakfast,' Hatcher grinned.

'Let's assume it is them. We'll go and take a look. We will ride down off the trail and swing in from the south. Leave the horses tied. All I want is Buckland. The others are of no concern to me,' Mondell said excitedly and began to sweat.

Hatcher ran his tongue round his lips. 'Right!' he agreed and followed Mondell off the trail, the thought of a large steak and a glass of beer in El Centro uppermost in his mind.

Devane was stretched out on the ledge using his fieldglasses. He shaded them with his hat so as not to let the sun reflect from them. He spotted the two riders who had halted on the hill crest. One horse was a roan and he was sure Hatcher was the rider. The other rider was using fieldglasses and he was sure it was Mondell. In a moment they moved off the trail and were just flashes of colour as they came on through the scrub bush. Devane got down quickly. 'They're coming!' he called to Hawk.

Hawk took the coffee pot off the fire and threw the dregs onto it. 'Here, Jonas, take this with you and stay with the horses out of sight,' he said sternly. 'Keep the revolver handy and do not hesitate to shoot, my friend, if either of those two get near.'

Buckland looked pallid and his hand shook as he took a grip on the revolver butt. He was certain he could not fire it, even in self-defence.

Revising his plan a little, Devane went down behind some rocks at the south side of the grove after telling Hawk to get up on the ledge to watch the east. Using the glasses he watched the riders as they halted at a stand of small trees by some rocks. He grinned. If he could get to the horses and free them, that would put those two afoot. They would not be easily caught if he took them up the trail a few miles. He could see Hatcher now checking his piece. Mondell had a rifle with him, and wore a side-gun. This was it, the showdown. It had been like this in Mexico three years ago, but there had been almost thirty soldiers after him then. He began to sweat a little.

Devane got up and ran to the foot of the boulder where Hawk lay. 'When they get closer fire off some shots at them. Keep them busy. I'm going to get their horses. It we put them afoot they won't catch up with us. A stage comes through sometime, so they won't die out here.'

Hawk nodded and felt the dryness in his mouth. He was no real hand with a gun. He would stop them getting to Jonas, if he had to kill them both, he told himself.

As Mondell came on scrambling from one bush to another, or a rock, Devane lay hidden and watched him go past, Some moments later he slithered away heading for the tethered horses.

Hatcher was not as careful as Mondell, he stood up by a bush and shaded his eyes as he stared at the rock formation. He could see a gap and a tiny wisp of smoke spiralling upwards from inside the boulders. He ran crouched over. He figured he would get in there and blast off. That would scatter whoever was in there. Mondell was coming up from the other side. It ought to be over soon. He flopped down as he heard a horse nicker from across the trail. So, that was where the horses were, he thought. He got up again. Suddenly a shot rang out and dust kicked up a yard away from his feet. 'Christ!' he swore. 'Should have knowed they wasn't that stupid.'

Mondell squashed himself down behind a small bush when he heard the shot. He also swore. They had been watching all the time. It must be Carruthers, he thought. He remembered last year how he had come out quite suddenly from behind a cactus bush and with his own horse. Too late he realized his mistake of leaving the horses. He looked back towards the place where they were tethered. He couldn't see if they were still there. The rifle spoke again, then a revolver. Hatcher must be in trouble. Damn him! Where was John Benedict hiding? Buckland, as he was now. That was the name he had implanted in his mind. He got up and ran to the outer circle of boulders. Slowly he slid around a large one till he could see into the grove. He saw what looked like the back of someone sitting next to a rock. He smiled. A dummy, a lure. By God this Carruthers was a smart fellow. He must have been in the army.

Hatcher was cursing as he could not move. He was pinned down. Where the hell was Mondell? Why didn't he give him some support? There seemed to be only one person firing. Perhaps one of them had stayed behind while the others went on. Buckland wouldn't be here. He cursed himself for not having ridden on yesterday, and got ahead of them.

Mondell was also thinking there was no more than one gunman. He ran swiftly across the grassy patch and came up behind a small boulder at the foot of a taller one. He could see out through a gap. Way across some three hundred yards away was a rider and he was leading a spare horse. His own horse, damn it. Soon he would be circling round and he would most likely have a rifle.

A shot rang out from over his head and he jumped. Then he saw the stab of fire from Hatcher's revolver in reply. He was out there on the ground pinned down. He must get the one on top of the rock. Quickly he ran back again to the other side of the grove and got down between two rocks. Up on the ledge he could see a leg sticking out from behind a slab. He took out his Colt and fired at the rock above the leg. He heard a curse and the leg was drawn in. He had the man trapped. Now Hatcher could move while he kept the man busy. If he had to kill him then so be it.

Devane urged the horses along through the scrub circling in from the north side. He could see Hatcher and hear him firing. He could also see Buckland as he stood waving and pointing. He put his heels into the roan and went racing down towards Buckland. He threw himself out of the saddle at his feet. 'Tie these two up with the others and don't let them get away. Hawk needs help,' he shouted, then he ran across the track coming in on the west side of the boulders.

Hawk was lying low between the slab and the rock face. He knew he was in a tight spot now. He watched Hatcher get up and sprint in towards the boulders. He squeezed off a shot. Hatcher suddenly staggered and yelled. He went down and lay flat as Hawk put another shot in front of him. Then he turned over as a shot ricocheted off the slab, sending rock splinters all over him.

Hatcher was lying in agony, his leg oozing blood from above the knee. He pulled his bandanna from his neck and got it tied above the wound. Then he started hauling himself towards the rocks as he heard Mondell's Colt firing. This was something he hadn't foreseen. It had not occurred to him he might get shot.

Maybe those three in there, or two, were trail bums. Maybe it wasn't Buckland and his friends after all. Two ex-cons couldn't be in such good fettle. He got to the rocks and pulled himself in sitting with his back to them. He could do nothing now. He wasn't going to die for that bastard Mondell.

Mondell knew he had the man trapped. He wasn't firing any more. He called out to him. 'You might as well come on down. I don't wish to kill you.'

Devane had got inside the grove. He heard no more shots. Then he heard Mondell's voice and saw him stand up. Very quickly he sprinted across the grassy space and was up behind Mondell before he realized what had happened. He heard cloth rubbing against the rock and swung round, only to meet the rifle stock that swung up under his jaw. He fell against the rock and slumped down in a heap.

'Sorry, Louis!' Devane grinned. 'But you should always watch your back. Didn't they teach you that in the army?'

Hawk poked his head up over the slab

which had saved him from extinction. He hastily crossed himself, and seeing Devane below scrambled down and ran quickly across to him. 'Ay, ay! You are very good, amigo! I think he would have killed me if you hadn't come so fast.'

'Where's the other one?' Devane asked quietly.

'I put a bullet in his leg. He has crawled in to the rocks I think. He can still shoot though.'

'Go get some rope to tie this one up, and tell Jonas not to worry. I'll go flush Hatcher out.'

Hatcher was no trouble. He sat feeling sorry for himself with his back to the rock face. 'You get him?' he asked Devane who watched him closely.

'Your friend is out cold, if that is who you mean,' Devane answered evenly. 'He should have watched his back.' He took Hatcher's revolver and emptied the last two bullets from their chambers. 'Let me look at that leg. Just a flesh wound, you're lucky,' he told Hatcher who glared at him.

Hawk came then looking relieved. He spoke in Spanish and Devane answered him likewise.

When Mondell came round some fifteen minutes later he was trussed up hand and foot. He looked with hate at the man he knew as Carruthers. He also gave Fernandez a raking over. Where was Buckland? Had they made a mistake? Inside he was so furious he could have spat blood. To have been taken so was the most appalling humiliation. All he had thought about was getting Buckland. Now he was tied up like a chicken and they were gloating, he could see that. Hatcher was looking miserable and was wounded. He would be of no more use to him.

Devane brought their two canteens off their horses and the saddlebags and a sack with some food in it. 'A stage coach comes through most days. I don't know which way you are travelling, but you will be rescued before the water and food runs out. I will leave some ammunition up the trail under a rock and place a stick near it so you will find it. I don't know what you intended when you came in like you did. You are lucky to be still alive!'

Mondell did not speak. Nor did Hatcher. They sat there in sullen fury as Devane walked off. A few moments later they heard hoofbeats going west along the trail. Mondell was still tied up and could not get up to see if there were three men riding away. Hatcher did not even try. He would not get the other half of his money now, he was thinking, and he would be laid up for at least a couple of weeks in some flop house in El Centro if he should get there.

By the time darkness came, Devane pulled up in front of a trading post which was but a few miles from El Centro and at a fork in the trail. All three were about done in, especially Buckland. He was though greatly relieved that Mondell was unlikely to catch up with them now. He was also glad there had been no killing, and especially happy that he had not had to come face to face with him. Surely now he would go home and forget his paranoia about killing him.

Just to sit at a table and order a

proper meal was a treat in itself for the two ex-prisoners. Devane watched them devour the stew which he thought rather tough, and was probably goat meat, with amusement. He envied these two their friendship. It was the one good thing that had resulted from the awful catastrophe that had hit them without real cause. No one could imagine what they had gone through in that hell hole of a place. He got up and went to see the owner of the trading post and stage-line halt. He gave him a rather vague story about the two horses he wished to leave behind, explaining that two men might come along tomorrow or the next day and claim them. He left the swayback and took the roan for Hawk. He paid Pat Brady twenty dollars for looking after them. If Mondell and Hatcher didn't show Brady would have gained two horses, one of which, he suspected, would go into the stew pot. He chuckled at the thought of Hatcher and Mondell back there holding down their fury. He also began to think they might have been lucky and perhaps got a lift on a wagon or something. Reluctantly he told the other two they should move on and find a place up the northerly track which he saw from a rough map hanging on a wall would lead them to the railroad north of El Centro, and which ran to Bakersfield. From there they could go on to San Francisco.

Hawk and Jonas saw the good sense in his plan and wearily got into their saddles again. The horses had not, in fact, been pushed the last few days and with his new mount, Hawk was much happier.

Three days later, Marcus Kingsley received a telegraph from Bakersfield which told him the goods had arrived safely and that he should inform their despatcher. He knew immediately that John Benedict was free and sent word via the usual channels to his father. He felt a great relief. His part in it was over.

When the stage-coach slid to a halt along the trail going westwards, the driver got down to give a hand to help Hatcher up inside. There were only two other passengers. Mondell said little and simply handed over the money for the fares. When they came to the trading post, he was feeling none too well. Hatcher had complained a great deal. He would be glad to be rid of him. He had made up his mind he would not try to find Buckland. He would be miles away now. He might well never have been with Carruthers. It might have been just a decoy manoeuvre.

Brady gave Mondell and Hatcher a discerning look. He was sure these were the two the fella with those scrawny looking characters had mentioned. 'You the two as lost your horses?'

Mondell gave him a sharp look as he paid for a bottle of whiskey. 'Yes we lost them. Trail robbers jumped us and left us out there to die,' he said bitterly, as Hatcher added his scathing remarks.

'Well they wasn't trail bums, they left your horses with me. They're out back. It'll be five bucks for two days' keep,' Brady told Mondell.

Mondell went out to the corral with Brady. When he saw the sway back he gave a brief smile. Hatcher was going to be furious.

After Brady offered Hatcher ten dollars for the ageing horse, he calmed down a little. The stage driver got him back into the coach. Mondell said he would ride to El Centro and managed to sell his horse there. The following day he boarded the train for Los Angeles with bitter thoughts about his failure.

Devane, Fernandez and Buckland were in a state of euphoria as they sat in the cafe in Monterey. For almost a week they had slept and lazed in the quiet confines of one Carlos Carrera's hacienda, who was an old friend of Hawk's late father. They had eaten good and simple food, and swum in the ocean to get rid of the stench of Yuma Prison. Jonas had sent a long letter to Marcus Kingsley and had the money transferred for Pike, plus the telegraph as arranged. His father would soon know he was safe. Now what he had to do was decide where to go and what to do. Whatever it was he wanted his friends to be with him.

'I think it is possible that Mondell will go to Los Angeles and then to San Francisco. Then he will go home. He will not know where to search next.' Devane gave his considered view.

Buckland agreed. 'We could go up north and pan for gold. If you are staying with us. Later we can start up a restaurant in San Francisco. What about The Tres Hobos for a title?' he grinned widely.

Hawk picked up the large pacific prawn from the plate. 'What about The Last Prawn?' he said.

Devane laughed. 'One thing for sure. We won't be serving beans.'

This Large Print Book for the Partially sighted, who cannot read normal print, is published under the auspices of

THE ULVERSCROFT FOUNDATION

Other DALES Western Titles In Large Print

ELLIOT CONWAY
The Dude

JOHN KILGORE
Man From Cherokee Strip

J. T. EDSON
Buffalo Are Coming

ELLIOT LONG
Savage Land

HAL MORGAN
The Ghost Of Windy Ridge

NELSON NYE
Saddle Bow Slim